打開話匣子
——Small Talk一下！

L.J. Link
Nozawa Ai

著　何信彰　譯

三民書局

打開話匣子 —Small Talk 一下!

Contents

1. 天氣大家談／2
   WHY EVERYBODY TALKS ABOUT THE WEATHER

2. 日本生意人很無趣嗎？／8
   DO PRETTY GIRLS THINK JAPANESE BUSINESS-MEN ARE BORING?

3. 衣索比亞在華府？／14
   ETHIOPIA IN WASHINGTON D.C.?

4. 壽司的和風不再／20
   MAYBE SUSHI ISN'T JAPANESEY TODAY

5. 在東京買車／28
   BUYING A CAR IN TOKYO

6. 純種乎？雜種乎？／34
   PROBLEMS OF PURITY

7. 日出之國的遊戲規則／40
   DOES THE SUN RISE BY DIFFERENT RULES?

8. 曖昧的美德／46
   CRYSTAL CLEAR ANSWERS AREN'T ALWAYS THE BEST

9. 日本食物用英文怎麼說？／54
   HOW TO TALK ABOUT JAPANESE FOOD

10. 賭博？投資？／62
    GAMBLING VS. INVESTING

11. 約會：兩個幾乎沒有交集的人／70
DATING: TWO PEOPLE WHO HAVE LITTLE IN COMMON

12. 東京早晨的人潮／78
PROBLEMS OF THE MORNING RUSH IN TOKYO

13. 好人做到底／84
HOW TO BE A GOOD GUY

14. 淺談教會／90
WHAT TO DO AT CHURCH

15. 成田機場的老問題／98
THE PERENNIAL PROBLEM OF NARITA

16. 露營與杓子／106
HISHAKU AND CAMPING

17. 清談／114
THE VERY PINK OF A CONVERSATION

18. 淡季比較好玩?／120
IS OFF-SEASON MORE FUN?

19. 採買春酒飲料／126
DRINKS FOR AN AFTER-NEW YEAR'S PARTY

20. 店長難為／132
A MANAGER PUTS HIS FOOT IN HIS MOUTH

COMPREHENSION QUIZZES／140

給讀者的話

　　想和外國人打開話匣子Small Talk嗎？本書的目的就是要助你一臂之力。一般人都知道可以和外國人談一談自己的姓名、工作、家庭狀況、家住哪裡等等，不過接下來要聊什麼呢？仔細學習過本書對話之後，你的交談技巧必能有所精進，也能和外國人打開話匣子。

　　本書中的對話儘可能做到臨場感十足，並時而語帶詼諧。全書都是兩個人在特定場合中的對話，這種對話有其缺點，卻也有其優點，缺點在於如此一來，可能很難把此一特定場合中的對話，轉用在你本身的情況；優點則在於，現實中的對話，正是這樣你來我往。也許你會看到一些省略的措辭，甚至一些看起來有點奇怪的文法句構，但請你務必記得，學一些現實中沒有人講的對話，還不如不學。坊間充斥許多這一類的書，所用的詞句和對話只能在書中找到，現實生活中沒有人這樣說。學一學別人到底是怎麼交談的，就算有時候要多費一點苦功，也絕對有所幫助。你也會了解美國人心裡在想什麼，還有他們對於形形色色的外國文化有什麼看法。

　　每一則對話之後，都有關鍵句以及TIPS FOR EFFECTIVE COMMUNICATION（溝通實戰小祕訣），關鍵句對於大多數你會碰到的對話來說，都相當好用，你也會知道要怎麼使用這些句子，因為每一個句子都是從對話中節錄出來的。即使你只看關鍵句的部分，對於精進你的對話技巧，也可說是邁進了一大步。TIPS FOR EFFECTIVE COMMUNICATION則會解釋各種出處、參考資料、場合，以及文化背景，另外針對該則對話中某些措辭語句應該怎樣運用，也會加以說明。

　　另外有四則COFFEE BREAK（休息片刻）的單元，因為適切的成語、自然的用字、正確的語調固然重要，但要達到愉快有效

的溝通，則言辭以外的技巧也很重要，比方說對方在聆聽時我們要注意應有的手勢和說話的態度，這些因素深受文化制約，但說來奇怪，一般人卻常常忽略。不過本書沒有忘記這點，這四則COFFEE BREAK的單元，你可以仔細領略。

本書最後還針對每一則的對話，設計了一個簡易的COMPREHENSION QUIZZES（牛刀小試）單元，目的是測驗你對內容了解了多少，還有建議的ACTIVITY（讀後活動），你可能想用來一顯身手。

雖然關鍵字句的發音和音調都已標出，不過最好的方法還是在對話過程中，仔細聽一聽外籍老師的發音。為此，編輯部也準備了所有對話的CD，是本書最佳的輔助教材。

L. J. Link

2001年7月

給老師的話

看過「給讀者的話」裡頭列舉的理由，我們深信這些對話會是非常實用的教材，並在加以延伸後，也能變成作文的好題材，你也可以鼓勵學生用裡頭的關鍵句來造一些自己的句子。至於COMPREHENSION QUIZZES，要用來評分當然也可以，或是用來點明學生閱讀時應該注意的地方也可以。而建議的ACTIVITY適合會話課或是作文課，而且我們已經仔細分析過，一定能得到學生熱烈的反應。

打開話匣子
—Small Talk 一下!

1 天氣大家談
WHY EVERYBODY TALKS ABOUT THE WEATHER

Well, I hope we have better weather from now on.

Me too.

Wayne: Weather's not too bad today, is it?

Shinji: No, it isn't.

Wayne: Yeah, yesterday it was colder.

Shinji: It was, wasn't it?

Wayne: Well, I hope we have better weather from now on.

Shinji: Me too. I always feel better when the weather's good. Don't you?

Wayne: Yeah, I guess so.

Shinji: Do you always check the weather report?

Wayne: I guess I should.* But I don't. I don't know why but I don't.

Shinji: Me, I always check it. I don't know why but I always do.

Wayne: You remember what Mark Twain said? "Everybody always talks about the weather but no one does anything about it."

Shinji: Oh, did Mark Twain say that?

真治是東京一間貿易公司的新進營業員，剛和客戶開完會，正和同事一行人出去吃午餐，旁邊坐的是韋恩。

兩人之前其實見過面，不過沒有深入交談，只知道彼此的姓名。真治正煩惱怎麼找話題時，沒想到韋恩倒先開口了。兩人從天氣，一路聊到季節、興趣……，不知不覺聊了許多。

韋　恩：今天天氣還不錯喔？

真　治：是不錯。

韋　恩：對啊，昨天比較冷。

真　治：是啊，你也這麼覺得嗎？

韋　恩：嗯，我希望今天開始天氣就好轉。《from now on 從今以後》

真　治：我也希望是這樣，只要天氣一好，我的心情也會跟著好
　　　　起來，你也有這種感覺嗎？

韋　恩：嗯，我想應該是吧。

真　治：你都會看天氣預報嗎？

韋　恩：我應該要看，不過也不知道為什麼，就是沒有看。

真　治：我的話是一定會看，不知道為什麼，我每天都會注意天
　　　　氣。

韋　恩：馬克‧吐溫曾說過一句話，不曉得你知不知道？他說：
　　　　「每個人都在談天氣，卻沒有半個人對它採取什麼行動。」

真　治：喔，馬克‧吐溫有說過這句話嗎？

Wayne: Yes, he did. Anyway I think he did. But it's true, you know. Everybody always talks about the weather. We're talking about the weather right now.

Shinji: Oh, it's true all right. But why do you think everybody talks about the weather?

Wayne: **That's a good question.** I guess it's because the weather is always there. It's all around us.

Shinji: Well, that's one reason. Any others?

Wayne: People can't argue about the weather. I mean who is going to argue about if it's cold or warm? Either it is or it isn't.

Shinji: You're right, no arguments.

Wayne: And then, especially if you don't know someone, I mean, like, we don't really know each other, the weather's easy to talk about.

Shinji: Well, yes, it's easy to start a conversation. But can you really keep a conversation going by just talking about the weather? How long can you keep talking about the weather?

Wayne: **You got a point.** You could then move to talking about the seasons though.

Shinji: Which season do you like best?

Wayne: Gee, I don't really know. Fall, maybe. I like hiking and fall is the best time for tramping along trails.

Shinji: Have you done much hiking in Japan?

Wayne: Not much. I don't know where to go and I can't read the trail signs.

Shinji: I have a friend who loves to hike. Maybe I can get him to take you along sometime.

Wayne: **Sounds good. I'd appreciate it.**

Shinji: But he doesn't speak much English.

韋　恩：他有說過。管他的，我想他應該有說過。不過你不覺得
　　　　這句話說得很有道理嗎？每個人都在談天氣，像我們兩
　　　　個現在就在談天氣。《you know 你知道的》

真　治：喔，是沒錯啦，不過依你看，為什麼大家都在談天氣呢？

韋　恩：問得好，我想是因為天氣跑不了，就在我們四周。

真　治：嗯，這是其中一個原因，還有其他原因嗎？《Any others? =
　　　　Are there any other reasons?》

韋　恩：一般人不會因為談天氣就傷了和氣，我是說，沒有人會
　　　　因為天氣到底是冷是熱就吵了起來，反正不是冷就是熱。
　　　　《I mean 我的意思是》

真　治：你說得對，沒有人會爭這個。《no arguments = there will be no
　　　　arguments》

韋　恩：還有，尤其是你不太認識一個人的時候，我是說，就好
　　　　比我們兩個彼此不熟，也可以隨口聊上幾句天氣。《like 比
　　　　方說》

真　治：嗯，也對，聊天氣很容易就可以打開話匣子，可是只聊
　　　　天氣的話，真的能夠一直聊下去嗎？你談天氣能夠撐多
　　　　久呢？

韋　恩：你說到重點了，也許接下來你可以談一談四季。

真　治：你最喜歡哪一個季節？

韋　恩：喔，我也不是很清楚，可能是秋天吧。我喜歡健行，沿
　　　　著小路跋山涉水，秋天是最棒的時機。

真　治：你在日本走過很多地方嗎？

韋　恩：不是很多，我不知道要去哪裡，山路上的路標我也看不
　　　　懂。

真　治：我有一個朋友很喜歡健行，或許我可以請他找個時間帶
　　　　你一起去。

韋　恩：聽起來不錯，真是謝謝你。

真　治：不過他不太會講英文。

Wayne: **So what?** I don't speak much Japanese.

Shinji: Well, I don't know. He might feel uncomfortable. But his wife speaks English fairly well.

Wayne: Great. **Problem solved.**

Shinji: But, you see, his wifc never hikes.

Wayne: He never takes his wife hiking?

Shinji: I don't think so. I don't even know if she wants to hike. But in any case, he doesn't take her hiking.

Wayne: So our problem isn't solved?

Shinji: No, it looks like it isn't.

Wayne: Anyway, looks like lunch is over, and listen, it's been great meeting you.

Shinji: **Same here.** Hope to see you again.

關鍵句

That's a good question.	（這個問題）問得好。
You got a point.	（你說的）很有道理。／你說到重點了。
Sounds good.	聽起來不錯。／好極了。
I'd appreciate it.	謝謝你的幫忙。／真是謝謝你。
So what?	那又怎樣？
Problem solved.	問題解決了。
Same here.	我也有同感。／我也是。／我也一樣。

韋　恩：那又怎樣？我也不太會講日文。

真　治：嗯，不曉得耶，他可能會覺得不自在吧，不過他太太英文講得相當好。

韋　恩：太好了，問題解決了！《Problem solved. = The problem is solved.》

真　治：不過，你知道嗎，他太太從來不去健行。

韋　恩：他都沒有帶他太太一起去嗎？

真　治：應該沒有，我是不知道他太太喜不喜歡健行啦，不過從來都沒看過他帶他太太去健行。

韋　恩：所以問題還沒有解決囉？

真　治：沒錯，看來是還沒有。

韋　恩：不管了，我們的午餐差不多吃完了。對了，跟你聊天真的很愉快。

真　治：我也是，希望下次還有機會。

○ TIPS FOR EFFECTIVE COMMUNICATION ○

▶I guess I should. 很多人對於had better～似乎情有獨鍾，以為所有「應該～比較好」的句型都可以套用，其實不是這麼回事。例如，在路上遇到有人問路：「要到池袋的話，要搭地下鐵還是山手線？」這時就該回答"You should [It's better to] take the Yamanote Line.",而不是"You had [You'd] better take the Yamanote Line."。後者語氣帶有Or something terrible will happen.(否則你會倒大楣)，問路的外國人可能會被你嚇一跳。有些人以為You should～的語氣過於強硬，其實正好相反，像是本文的會話中就不能說"I guess I had better."。

2 日本生意人很無趣嗎?
DO PRETTY GIRLS THINK JAPANESE BUSINESSMEN ARE BORING?

Linda: Excuse me, would you know where the Hama Art Gallery is?

Yoshiro: The Hama Gallery? That's where I'm going too. My friend is showing some pictures there. **I'll take you.** It's not far.

Linda: That's lucky, thanks. I guess you like art.

Yoshiro: Yes, I like paintings. Oil paintings.

Linda: I'm an art student, myself, and **I wanted to see** the arts of Japan **with my own eyes**. But to make a little money, I'm teaching English.

Yoshiro: By the way, where do you teach?

Linda: I don't teach at a school. I work for a company that farms me out to different Japanese companies. So I usually teach Japanese businessmen. And it ain't much fun.* I had a long tough morning and I feel like a sponge somebody's wrung out.

Yoshiro: The gallery is just around this corner. But if you're tired, how about some coffee before we go in? (*pointing to a coffee shop*) This is a nice place.

Linda: Why, thank you. That's a good idea.

Yoshiro: The pastries here are made by the owner himself.

Linda: Pastries? **With my sweet tooth,** I can't resist.

(*They go inside and order coffee and pastries.*)

琳達是美術學校的學生，二十歲，美國人，到日本將近半年，課餘時間在幾家貿易公司教英文賺生活費。這個週末下午，她到東京銀座看畫展，卻遲遲找不到畫廊的正確地址，只好向路人請教。路人伊勢喜郎是國際PR公司的部長，經常到美國出差。聽到琳達說「日本的生意人很無趣」，吃驚地細問原委……

琳　達：　對不起，你知道Hama（日文「海濱」之意）美術館在哪
　　　　　裡嗎？

喜　郎：　Hama美術館嗎？我也正要去那裡，我朋友在那邊展出一
　　　　　些畫，我帶妳去，離這裡不遠。《be showing 正在展覽》

琳　達：　運氣真好，謝謝你了，我猜你一定很喜愛藝術。

喜　郎：　是啊，我喜歡繪畫作品，油畫。

琳　達：　我本身是學美術的，我一直想要親眼見識日本的藝術，
　　　　　不過我也在教英文，賺一點錢。

喜　郎：　順便問一下，妳在哪裡教英文？

琳　達：　我不是在學校教，我是替一家公司工作，他們會派我到
　　　　　很多家日本公司去教英文，通常對象都是日本生意人，
　　　　　不過不是很有趣。今天早上的時間就過得特別慢，很不
　　　　　好過，感覺好像被榨乾的海綿。《ain't = is not〔俚語〕》

喜　郎：　美術館就在轉角的地方，不過如果妳累了，要不要先去
　　　　　喝杯咖啡再進去看展覽？（指著一家咖啡店）這家店還不
　　　　　錯。

琳　達：　哇，謝謝你，這個點子不錯。

喜　郎：　這家店的糕點是店長手工做的。《pastries 糕點》

琳　達：　糕點嗎？我最喜歡吃甜食了，我沒辦法抗拒。

（他們走進店裡，點了咖啡和糕點。）

Yoshiro: Now, tell me why you don't like teaching Japanese businessmen.

Linda: Oh, I don't know. I guess it's because it's so boring.

Yoshiro: Boring?

Linda: It's boring because they don't say much. And then, maybe half of them don't really want to study; it's their company that wants them to study.

Yoshiro: Well, what do you teach them?

Linda: Oh, you know. "How are you?" And how to order food in a restaurant and how to buy plane tickets and how to ask directions. **The usual stuff.**

Yoshiro: That doesn't sound too interesting.

Linda: It sure isn't. **It bores the hell out of me.**

Yoshiro: Well, if you're bored and if the material you are teaching is boring, isn't it natural the students are bored?

Linda: I suppose so. But I have to use the textbook they give me. Oh well. By the way, what do you do?

Yoshiro: I'm afraid to tell you. I'm a businessman.

Linda: Oh, I'm sorry. I didn't mean that every Japanese businessman is **as dead as a doornail**. I didn't mean that at all.

Yoshiro: I know. Maybe we should be getting to the gallery. And I hope you won't think all Japanese businessmen are boring.

Linda: I don't know about all Japanese businessmen, but you are certainly anything but boring. You know, you never told me your name. Mine's Linda, Linda Thompson.

Yoshiro: My name is Ise, Yoshiro Ise. Nice to meet you Miss Thompson.

Linda: Just call me Linda.

Yoshiro: O.K., Linda.

喜　郎：可以說一說為什麼妳不喜歡教日本的生意人嗎？

琳　達：喔，我也不知道，我想是因為很無聊吧！
喜　郎：很無聊？
琳　達：因為他們課堂上都不大發言，所以很無聊，還有啊，可能有一半的人不是真的很想學吧，是他們的公司要他們學的。
喜　郎：嗯，那妳教他們什麼？
琳　達：喔，就是「你好嗎？」之類的。還有如何在餐廳點菜、如何買機票、如何問路等等，都是一般性的題材。

喜　郎：聽起來也不是很有趣。
琳　達：沒錯，無聊斃了。
喜　郎：嗯，假如妳都覺得無聊，而且教材真的也很枯燥的話，那學生覺得無趣不是理所當然的事嗎？
琳　達：應該是吧，可是我得用他們拿給我的教科書，喔，對了，那你是做什麼的？
喜　郎：我不是很想說，因為我就是生意人。
琳　達：喔，真是不好意思，我不是說每個日本生意人都像木頭似的，我絕對沒有這個意思。
喜　郎：我知道。也許我們應該去展覽會場了，我希望妳不會覺得日本每個生意人都很無聊。
琳　達：我也不是很了解所有的日本生意人啦，不過你絕對不是無聊的人。對了，你還沒跟我說你的名字呢，我叫琳達，琳達‧湯普生。
喜　郎：我叫伊勢，伊勢喜郎，很高興認識妳，湯普生小姐。

琳　達：叫我琳達就可以了。
喜　郎：好的，琳達。

關鍵句

I'll take you.	我帶你去。
I want to see ～ with my own eyes.	我想要親眼見識～。
With my sweet tooth,	我喜歡吃甜食
The usual stuff.	一般性的題材。／常見的教材。
It bores the hell out of me.	非常無聊。／無聊斃了。
As dead as a doornail	〔片語〕完全僵死的／像塊木頭似的

12

○ TIPS FOR EFFECTIVE COMMUNICATION ○

▶ it ain't much fun 「不是很有趣」 are not, am not的縮寫原本是an't，在西元1800年左右改為ain't，如今主要作為下列用法的俚語縮寫：am not (I ain't going to school.), have not (I ain't got a pencil.), are not (My friends ain't going to school either.)，以及本文會話中所表示的is not的縮寫。

ain't經常出現在熟人之間的對話，中下階層的人尤其愛用，連帶給人一種「沒教養、教育程度低」的印象，電影中出身低微的角色便常常使用這個字。因此，英、美、加地區的人為了不想被認為沒有教養，不少人拒絕使用ain't，這對於把英語當外語學習的人來說，當然也最好避免，省得被當成了呆子。另外，在會話中，琳達是以開玩笑的語氣，故意用ain't來強調「無趣」。

▶ With my sweet tooth 這裡的tooth指的不是牙齒，而是對食物的喜好。有句慣用語"I have a sweet tooth."，意思就是「我喜歡吃甜食」。

3 衣索比亞在華府?
ETHIOPIA IN WASHINGTON D.C.?

James: **Long time no see.*** When did you get back?

Rob: Sunday night. Just in time to get back to work today. **What a drag.**

James: Your trip?

Rob: No, no. Work. Getting back to work. The trip was great!

James: Where'd you go? D.C., wasn't it?

Rob: Right. D.C. My brother, he's a doctor, he lives there. His neighborhood is filled with Ethiopians.

James: Ethiopians?

Rob: Well, I was surprised myself. There are more Ethiopians in his section per square foot than in any other place outside of Ethiopia.

James: That's funny.

Rob: I know it's funny. That's why I'm mentioning it. I took a walk with Sally down 18th Street and saw an Ethiopian restaurant and I said to Sally, "Hey, an Ethiopian restaurant, let's try it for lunch." We keep walking and in ten minutes we saw ten Ethiopian restaurants. Couldn't believe it.

羅伯和詹姆士都是在東京某證券公司任職的美國人，羅伯三十歲，詹姆士三十五歲，到日本同樣快居滿五年。兩人不只是同事，私底下交情也不錯。

羅伯之前請了兩個星期的長假，昨晚剛回來，今天中午便邀詹姆士一起吃午餐。他說他在華府看到很多非洲、中東等地的餐館，有條街上竟然開了十多家的衣索比亞餐館。他走進其中一家用餐……

詹姆士： 好久不見，什麼時候回來的？

羅　伯： 星期天晚上，恰好趕得回來上今天的班，真是煩人。

詹姆士： 旅行很煩人？

羅　伯： 不是，不是旅行，是工作。旅行很不錯，是回來工作很煩人。

詹姆士： 你去哪裡？不是去華府嗎？ (D.C. = Washington D.C.)

羅　伯： 沒錯，就是華府，我弟弟是醫生，他就住在那邊，他家附近到處都是衣索比亞人。

詹姆士： 衣索比亞人？

羅　伯： 對啊，我自己也很驚訝，那個地方每平方英尺單位面積的衣索比亞人口數，僅次於衣索比亞當地。

詹姆士： 真是不可思議。 (funny 不可思議的)

羅　伯： 我就是覺得很不可思議，所以才會講出來。我和莎莉在十八街散步，突然看到一家衣索比亞餐廳，我就跟莎莉說：「嘿，衣索比亞餐廳耶！午餐時就吃這一家好了。」後來我們又繼續往下走，結果十分鐘之內，就看到十家衣索比亞餐廳，真是令人難以置信。

James: Well, how was the food?

Rob: We didn't have lunch there that day. If there had been only one Ethiopian restaurant, we would have eaten there. No problem. But with more than ten, we couldn't decide which one to go to, so we didn't go that day.

James: Well, did you go to one of those restaurants eventually or not?

Rob: Oh we did. We did. First I asked a cab driver which restaurant he'd recommend. He said he was from Nigeria and never ate that food because it was too spicy and besides, he had an ulcer.

James: **Sounds like you struck gold.** So what did you do?

Rob: Well, later we went to a bookshop and I asked the guy there and he suggested a particular place and that's where we went.

James: How was the food?

Rob: Oh the food was fine. Unusual and tasty. That wasn't the problem.

James: What was the problem?

Rob: The problem was eating it.

James: The food was good but you couldn't eat it? **I don't follow.***

Rob: Oh we could eat it, **once we got the hang of it**. But it wasn't easy. You know how you eat Indian curries with some of that nan bread?

James: Sure. You mean they gave you some bread to eat it with?

Rob: **It was** bread **all right**. But it was soft, thin floppy bread. You couldn't use it to scoop up the food. What you had to do was rip off a piece, hold it between two fingers and then grab the food between the bread which was hard to do because I could only grab a small amount. Little by little I got better but it was really frustrating at first.

詹姆士：那菜色怎麼樣？

羅　伯：那一天我們沒有去那裡吃午餐，假如只有那麼一家衣索比亞餐廳的話，我們就會去那裡吃，一定會去的。不過後來出現了十多家，我們真不曉得要去哪一家，所以那天我們就沒有去吃。

詹姆士：那結果到最後你們有沒有去吃呢？

羅　伯：喔，有啊，有去吃。一開始我們問了一個計程車司機，問他覺得哪一家比較好吃，他說他是從奈及利亞來的，沒有吃過衣索比亞的食物，因為太辣了，而且他有胃潰瘍。

詹姆士：聽起來你還真是問對人了呢！〔反諷〕那後來你們怎麼辦？

羅　伯：嗯，後來我們就去一家書店，問那裡的店員，他推薦我們去一家很特別的店，我們就去了。

詹姆士：菜色怎麼樣？

羅　伯：喔，菜色還不錯，非常特別，蠻好吃的，不過問題不在菜色。

詹姆士：那問題是什麼？

羅　伯：吃的時候才有問題。

詹姆士：菜色很好，不過卻不能吃？我聽不懂。

羅　伯：喔，是可以吃，只是要等到我們抓到訣竅，不過不是很簡單，你知道要怎樣吃印度咖哩配nan麵包吧？

詹姆士：當然知道啊，你是說他們給你一些麵包配著吃？

羅　伯：是麵包沒錯，不過他們給的麵包又軟又薄，鬆鬆垮垮的，沒辦法把食物舀起來，只好撕一片下來，用兩根手指拿住，然後趕快用撈的把料撈到麵包中間，很不好弄，我只能撈一點點而已，後來慢慢就比較會了，不過一開始真的很令人氣餒。

James: O.K. **I get the picture.** What I really miss are the big deli sandwiches* stacked so thick you can barely open your mouth wide enough to bite on them.

Rob: Yeah,* those are great. And they're cheap.

James: Not like this lunch. But today, just today, **I'll get the check.**

Rob: I'm not going to protest. Many thanks. And we're off to the office.

關鍵句

Long time no see.	好久不見。
What a drag.	令人煩透了。 ／真是無聊。／無聊透頂。
Sounds like you struck gold.	聽起來你還真是問對人了呢。(直譯:聽起來像是你挖到了金礦。)
I don't follow.	我聽不懂。／我不了解。
Once we got the hang of it	一旦抓到竅門之後
It was~all right.	是~沒錯。(只是……)
I get the picture.	我知道是怎麼一回事了。
I'll get the check.	我請客。

詹姆士：　這樣喔，那我知道是怎麼一回事了。我最懷念的還是熟
　　　　　食店的超大三明治，疊了很多層，厚到嘴巴幾乎要塞不
　　　　　下。

羅　伯：　沒錯，很好吃，又很便宜。

詹姆士：　不像這頓午餐，不過今天，就今天喔，我請客。

羅　伯：　那我就不拒絕你的美意，謝謝你了。我們也應該回辦公
　　　　　室了。

○ TIPS FOR EFFECTIVE COMMUNICATION ○

▶ Long time no sée.　I haven't seen you for a long time.的口語
說法，常見於許久不見的熟人之間，要注意重音在see。

▶ I don't follow.　「菜色很好，不過卻不能吃？」邏輯有點怪怪
的，所以說「我跟不上你的邏輯」，意思是「聽嘸（聽不懂）」。

▶ deli sandwiches　deli (delicatessen)是專賣三明治等熟食的
小吃店，店裡賣的三明治中間夾的料非常多，像是起司、火腿、
臘腸、生菜等等，分量十足，非常好吃。相較起來，日本賣的
三明治就顯得單薄了，在美國人眼中，根本吃不到什麼東西。

▶ Yeah　「是啊」　許多初學者喜歡用yeah代替yes，經常不看
對象、場合，鬧了笑話也不知道。要注意，不是任何時候，yes
都可以用yeah來代替的。

4 壽司的和風不再
MAYBE SUSHI ISN'T JAPANESEY TODAY

Avis: O.K. Mr. Suzuki. **I'm all set.**

Keisuke: Great. What would you like to have for lunch?

Avis: Something real Japanesey.* You decide. The only thing I don't want is hamburger or steak or Kentucky Fried Chicken.

Keisuke: You don't want steak?

Avis: Absolutely not. Wouldn't it be a terrible waste to eat steak in Japan when I can get steak anytime back home? I want something real Japanesey.

Keisuke: Japanesey?

Avis: I mean something that you'd only find in Japan.

Keisuke: **No problem.** I know. We'll have sushi.

Avis: Mr. Suzuki. You know we can get sushi in America. I want food I can't get back home.

Keisuke: No problem. I know. We'll have sukiyaki.

Avis: Mr. Suzuki. Please. Sukiyaki and tempura* and sushi and tofu, why, every Japanese restaurant in America has those.

Keisuke: Well, just a minute, let me think.

Avis: How about blowfish?

Keisuke: Blowfish? What is that?

Avis: Don't you know what blowfish is? Somebody told me it's a real Japanese delicacy and that it's dangerous. It has a special poison and if you eat it, you die.

　　愛維絲是美國維吉尼亞州的國貿局代表，目前正在日本訪問，預計停留兩個禮拜。這是她第一次到日本，目的是希望吸引更多的日本企業到維吉尼亞州投資。這天，她來到東京一家大企業的總公司拜訪，鈴木圭介是該公司纖維部的部長。結束上午的會商後，兩人打算去吃中餐，鈴木詢問愛維絲的意見……

愛維絲：好了，鈴木先生，我準備好了。《be all set 準備好了》

圭　介：太好了，那妳中午要吃什麼？

愛維絲：你決定吧，很有日本風味就行了，只要不是漢堡、牛排或是肯德基炸雞就好。

圭　介：妳不要吃牛排喔？

愛維絲：當然不要，我回國的話，什麼時候想吃牛排都可以，來日本還吃牛排不是很浪費嗎？我要吃點名副其實的日本風味。《back home 回國》

圭　介：日本風味？

愛維絲：我是說只能在日本吃得到的東西。

圭　介：沒問題，我知道了，那吃壽司好了。

愛維絲：鈴木先生，你知道我們在美國也可以吃到壽司吧，我要吃一些我在美國吃不到的東西。

圭　介：沒問題，我知道了，我們可以去吃壽喜燒。

愛維絲：拜託，鈴木先生，壽喜燒和天婦羅，還有壽司、豆腐，唉呀，美國的日本料理店就有這些東西了。

圭　介：這樣喔，等一等，讓我想一下。

愛維絲：我們去吃blowfish好不好？

圭　介：Blowfish？這是什麼東西？

愛維絲：你不知道blowfish喔？有人跟我說這是道地的日本美食耶，可是很危險，有一種特別的毒，吃了就會死翹翹。

Keisuke: Blowfish? Poison? Oh, you mean *fugu*. *Fugu*? You want to eat *fugu*?

Avis: If *fugu* is blowfish and if it's dangerous to eat, that's what I want.

Keisuke: Ms. Meyers, I'm a little surprised. But if you are serious, we can have *fugu*.

Avis: Wonderful. All my friends will **be green with envy**.

Keisuke: But, Ms. Meyers, I just realized that we can't have *fugu* today because **it is out of season**.

Avis: Out of season?

Keisuke: Yes, *fugu* is only served in the winter and not in the summer.

Avis: **What a blow!** No blowfish. Ha! Ha!

Keisuke: What's so funny?

Avis: It's a joke. What a blow, no blowfish. We call that a pun.

Keisuke: I see. Well, let me think, what can we have? Maybe this is a long shot,* but how about *dojo*?

Avis: *Dojo*? What is that?

Keisuke: Just a minute. Let me get my dictionary. (*pause*) Loach. Yes, how about loach?

Avis: Roach? You eat roaches? Mr. Suzuki, I'm sorry but for Americans roaches are simply, well, disgusting. I couldn't eat that.

Keisuke: O.K. but it's just a very simple freshwater fish and it's grilled over charcoal.

Avis: Fish? Did you say fish? I thought you said roach. A roach isn't a fish.

圭　介：　Blowfish? 有毒？喔，你是說河豚（譯者按：fugu為河豚的日文發音）嗎？妳要吃河豚？

愛維絲：　如果河豚就是blowfish，而且吃河豚很危險的話，那就是我要吃的。

圭　介：　麥俄絲小姐，我有點嚇一跳，不過如果妳是認真的，那我們就吃河豚吧。

愛維絲：　太棒了，我朋友一定會嫉妒得半死。

圭　介：　但是，麥俄絲小姐，我剛剛才想到我們今天吃不到河豚，因為現在不是盛產期。

愛維絲：　不是盛產期？

圭　介：　沒錯，只有冬天才供應河豚，夏天沒有。

愛維絲：　What a blow! No blowfish. 哈！哈！

圭　介：　這有什麼好笑的嗎？

愛維絲：　只是開玩笑而已，What a blow, no blowfish. 這是雙關語。（譯者按：「真是晴天霹靂！居然沒有blowfish!」，此處套用blow的「晴天霹靂」之意的雙關語）

圭　介：　了解了，那這樣的話，我想一下還能吃什麼？雖然可能是大膽的嘗試，不過妳要不要去吃*dojo*（譯者按：dojo為泥鰍的日文發音)?

愛維絲：　*Dojo*? 那是什麼東西？

圭　介：　等一下，我拿一下字典。（過了一會）是泥鰍，沒錯，妳要不要去吃泥鰍？

愛維絲：　蟑螂？你們吃蟑螂？鈴木先生，很抱歉，我們美國人覺得蟑螂實在是，嗯，太噁心了，我不敢吃。

圭　介：　好吧，沒關係，不過那只是很普通的淡水魚，放在木炭上炭烤而已。

愛維絲：　魚，你是說魚嗎？我以為你說的是蟑螂，蟑螂又不是魚。

Keisuke: Of course it's a fish and maybe you don't have it in America.

Avis: **How do you spell it?**

Keisuke: L-O-A-C-H.

Avis: Oh. I'm sorry. I thought you said roach, R-O-A-C-H.

Keisuke: Roach? What's a roach? Let me get my dictionary. (*looking it up in the dictionary*) Oh no. No, no Japanese eats roaches. **It's all a mistake.**

Avis: Anyway, **I feel better now. It's all clear.** I love talking to people and communicating. Wait till I tell my friends back home. **They'll just die.**

Keisuke: Die?

Avis: I mean they'll die laughing.

Keisuke: They'll die laughing?

Avis: Mr. Suzuki, why don't we go eat loach?

Keisuke: I'm sorry for my poor English.

Avis: Don't be sorry. Your English is super. I just misheard you. Let's eat loach.

Keisuke: Ms. Meyers, it is now almost 12:30 because we have been talking a while. And if we go to have loach—which is far from here, we won't make it back in time for the 1:30 meeting.

Avis: That's too bad. Do you have a backup plan?

Keisuke: Steak. But before you object, it's Japanese steak that you can't get in America.

Avis: What's so special about Japanese steak?

Keisuke: Number one,* the cows are given beer. Number two,* a good Japanese steak is about $150.00.

Avis: A hundred fifty dollars! **You're kidding!** Let's go. That'll be something to write home about.

圭 介：當然是魚啊，可能是因為你們美國沒有吧。

愛維絲：怎麼拼？

圭 介：L-O-A-C-H。

愛維絲：喔，不好意思，我以為你說的是蟑螂，R-O-A-C-H。

圭 介：Roach? 什麼是roach? 我拿一下字典。(查一查字典)喔，
　　　天啊，不是啦，沒有日本人吃蟑螂的啦，這完全是一場
　　　誤會。

愛維絲：沒差啦，我現在覺得好多了，一切都弄清楚了，我喜歡
　　　和別人談天、交換意見，等我回國跟我朋友說，他們一
　　　定都會死掉。

圭 介：死掉？

愛維絲：我是說他們會笑得半死。

圭 介：笑得半死？

愛維絲：鈴木先生，可以去吃泥鰍了嗎？

圭 介：不好意思，我的英文很破。

愛維絲：沒什麼好不好意思的，你的英文一級棒，是我聽錯了，
　　　我們去吃泥鰍吧。

圭 介：麥俄絲小姐，快要十二點半了，我們剛才聊了一段時間，
　　　如果去吃泥鰍的話，離這邊很遠，就沒有辦法趕回來參
　　　加一點半的開會了。

愛維絲：真可惜，你有其他的打算嗎？

圭 介：牛排，不過在妳反對以前，我要說這是妳在美國吃不到
　　　的日式牛排。

愛維絲：日式牛排有什麼特別？

圭 介：第一，這牛是喝啤酒的；第二，上等的日式牛排大概要
　　　美金一百五十元。

愛維絲：一百五十元！ 不會吧！ 那就走吧，我寫信回家時可以記
　　　上這一筆。

4

關鍵句

I'm all set.	我都準備好了。
No problem.	沒問題。／好啊。
Be green with envy	嫉妒得半死
It is out of season.	現在不是盛產期。
What a blow!	好大的打擊！／真是晴天霹靂！
How do you spell it?	（這個字）怎麼拼？
It's all a mistake.	完全是一場誤會。
I feel better now.	（現在）感覺好多了。
It's all clear.	一切都搞清楚了。／真相大白了。／水落石出。
They'll just die.	他們會（笑）死掉。
You're kidding!	騙人的吧！／不會吧！／真的嗎？

FUGU

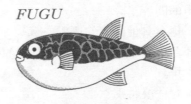

DOJO

○ TIPS FOR EFFECTIVE COMMUNICATION ○

▶Japanesey　也可以拼成Japanesy，是Japanesque的俚俗說法。像這樣直接在形容詞、名詞後面加上y，作「～風味／特色」解釋的情形，在英語中非常多。例如：cheapy（廉價的）、cheesey（像起司的）、goofy（愚蠢的）等等。

▶Sukiyaki and tempura...　「美國人只吃牛排和漢堡」這句話在十幾年前還可以成立，不過如今美國幾乎所有城市至少都有一、兩家日本料理店，壽喜燒、天婦羅、壽司等等，已經不再是什麼稀奇的菜色了。

▶Maybe this is a long shot　說這句話的心態其實是Probably it's not a good idea because you won't like it.（不是什麼好主意，因為我想你不會喜歡的），long shot指的是「（沒有把握的）猜測」或「（希望渺茫的）嘗試」。

▶Number one～. Number two...　說完自己的論點之後，用來補述理由的說法，意思是「第一～，第二……」，也可以說成A～，B....。例如："I don't like *natto*. Because, A: it smells awful, B: it's slimy."（我不喜歡納豆。原因是第一，它的味道很臭；第二，它黏黏的）。

5 在東京買車
BUYING A CAR IN TOKYO

Jack: Suppose you were getting a new car, what would you go for?

Don: I don't know. I like Honda. I like BMW. But there's a new model coming out every other month. Who knows?

Jack: I know there are new models. **I know that.** But what would you get?

Don: For Tokyo?

Jack: For Tokyo.

Don: Well, the first thing is, do you like an automatic or a 4-on-the-floor?

Jack: If I think about Tokyo traffic, an automatic is the way to go. But I like to take long weekend trips to the country, and for that, I'd rather have a manual.

Don: Well, which is it going to be? Personally, I'm for manual. Gives you more control. And keeps repair costs down.

Jack: Yeah, I guess manual is for me. Though automatics seem more popular. And, you know, I never could figure out why they put the shift on the floor. It used to be right up by the steering wheel. That's so much more convenient. And safer.

Don: They just don't make those anymore. And I'll tell you why. The old shifts with the lever by the steering column were clumsy and slow. They got a bad image. The shift on the floor evokes images of racing cars. So now, even automatics, have the shift lever on the floor, not because it's more practical, but because of the image. I

傑克和唐恩是美商銀行東京分行的同事，兩人都是美國人，年紀相仿，未婚，又幾乎同時期進入公司，私底下交情非常好。自從他們到東京工作以來，已經過了三個年頭。

某日在公司，傑克向唐恩說他想買車。唐恩對車子很熟，他傳授傑克買車前要注意哪些事項，傑克聽得目瞪口呆。

傑　克：假設你要買一部新車，你會偏好哪一種車？

唐　恩：我也不知道，我喜歡Honda，也喜歡BMW，不過每隔幾個月就會推出新的車款，誰知道？

傑　克：我知道會有新車款，我很清楚，不過你會買哪一部？

唐　恩：要在東京開嗎？

傑　克：對，在東京開。

唐　恩：嗯，首先要決定的就是，你喜歡自排還是手排？

傑　克：考慮到東京的交通，自排比較可行，不過我週末喜歡開車到鄉下去玩，這樣的話，我寧願買手排的。

唐　恩：嗯，要買哪一種呢？就我個人來說，我喜歡手排，操控性佳，修車費用也低。

傑　克：沒錯，我想手排比較適合我，雖然好像比較多人開自排車。還有，我老是搞不懂為什麼車商把排檔放在底盤，本來的排檔就在方向盤旁邊，那樣方便多了，而且也比較安全。

唐　恩：那種車已經沒有出了，告訴你為什麼好了，因為舊式的排檔桿就在方向盤旁邊，既不雅觀又遲鈍，給人的印象不好。排檔移到底盤，則給人有賽車的印象。所以現在，就算是自排車，排檔桿也在底盤，不是因為這樣比較好開，而是因為給人不同的印象。我的意思是說，你想想

mean, think about it. Before, in a pinch, three people could sit up front. Now, only two can and if you want to get out the other door, you've got to go through all kinds of contortions because that shift is on the floor.

Jack: You are *so* right. What beats triangle windows? Yet almost no cars have them anymore.

Don: Well, at least retractable headlights seem on the way out. What a farce that was.

Jack: A farce?

Don: An absolute farce. The rationale for those headlights was that they improved drag. You know, cut down on wind resistance to increase mileage.

Jack: Didn't they?

Don: Sure they did. When the lights were closed. But when they opened up, the drag was worse. And even closed, fuel efficiency was not increased because the weight of the motor easily canceled out any benefits.

Jack: Anyone who says technology is rational needs their head examined.

Don: A car's supposed to be transportation. But it's definitely become an image thing as well.

Jack: **That's unavoidable.** I admit I like a car to look good. And for Tokyo, I've got to have air-conditioning.

Don: **I don't blame you.** You know, of course, that's going to add a hefty amount to the price.

Jack: I know. But as we say in Chicago, no ginger.

Don: No ginger?

Jack: Yeah, no ginger. Never heard that expression?

Don: No ginger? **What in the name of creation is that?**

看嘛，以往必要時，前面可以坐三個人，現在，只能坐兩個人，而且假如你想要從另一邊的車門出來，你還得用盡方法扭曲身體，因為排檔就在底盤的位置。《steering column 方向盤承軸的部分／evoke 喚起》

傑　克：說得真透徹。還有，有什麼比得過三角窗（邊窗）呢？可是現在幾乎看不到了。

唐　恩：嗯，至少隱藏式車前燈慢慢消失了，那東西簡直是胡鬧。

傑　克：胡鬧？

唐　恩：真的是胡鬧，當初設計這種車前燈的理論依據是因為它們改善了阻力，就是可以減少風阻，增加行駛的哩程數。

傑　克：真的有嗎？

唐　恩：當然有，不過是車燈關著的時候。車燈打開之後，阻力就變大了，而且就算關著，燃料的效益也沒有增加，因為引擎的重量很輕易就抵消所有的優點。

傑　克：那些說科技很理性的人，他們的腦袋瓜都應該拿去檢查一下。

唐　恩：車子應該是用來運輸的，不過看來也跟形象扯上關係了。

傑　克：那是在所難免的。我承認我喜歡一部看起來很尊貴的車，而且要在東京開的話，還得裝空調。

唐　恩：也不怪你。不過想必你也知道那要多花很大一筆錢。

傑　克：我知道，不過就像我們芝加哥人說的，no ginger（沒辦法／不可能）。

唐　恩：No ginger?

傑　克：沒錯，no ginger，沒聽過這種講法嗎？

唐　恩：No ginger? 那到底是什麼東西？

Jack: *Shoganai.* Never heard that? *Shoga*, ginger, *nai*, no, nothing. Get it?

Don: Jack. Please. **Spare me.** Spare me.

Jack: Anyway, what car should I get?

Don: Of course, you've got a parking space, right?

Jack: A parking space? No, but I guess I can find one.

Don: What are you? JOTB?* Just off the boat? You don't have a parking space and you want to buy a car?

Jack: **What's the big deal?**

Don: What's the big deal? He wants to know what's the big deal? Look, I don't know where you've been living until now, but to make the understatement of the year, you have got a problem. Forget about worrying about what car to buy and start worrying about getting a legal parking place.

Jack: A legal parking place?

關鍵句

I know thát.	我很清楚。 / 我很了解。
That's unavoidable.	那是在所難免的。 / 那是無法避免的。
I don't blame you.	我不怪你。 / 也不能怪你。
What in the name of creation is that?	那是什麼玩意兒?
Spare me.	饒了我吧。
What's the big deal?	有什麼大不了的?

傑　克： *Shoganai*，沒聽過嗎？日文的*shoga*（辦法），就是指ginger；*nai*，意思就是no，了解了嗎？

唐　恩： 拜託，傑克，饒了我，饒了我吧。

傑　克： 不管這個了，我應該買什麼車才好呢？

唐　恩： 想必你有停車位了對吧？

傑　克： 停車位？沒有，不過我想我可以找到停車位。

唐　恩： 你是何等人物？JOTB嗎？剛到日本嗎？沒有停車位你還想要買車啊？

傑　克： 這有什麼大不了？

唐　恩： 有什麼大不了？ 你這個人想要知道有什麼大不了的嗎？這個嘛，我是不知道你之前都住在哪裡，不過保守說來，你麻煩大了，你也不用煩惱要買什麼車不車的，煩惱你怎樣取得合法停車位的問題吧！

傑　克： 合法停車位？

○ TIPS FOR EFFECTIVE COMMUNICATION ○

▶ JOTB？（形容詞）「你是剛來的啊？」　just off the boat的縮寫，直譯是「才剛下船」。據說從前（現在也是）移民一開始都是坐船來到美洲大陸， 先來的移民或是當地人於是以此稱呼。

6 純種乎？雜種乎？
PROBLEMS OF PURITY

John: Boy, I'm glad that meeting's over. I'm dog-tired.

Tsutomu: I agree. But we had a lot of business to go over.

John: If it were education business, I wouldn't mind so much. Most of it, though, seemed administrative detail to me.

Tsutomu: John, by this time, surely you know that it's unavoidable.

John: True. True. But **it gets to me**.

Tsutomu: Gets to you?

John: Yeah. It irritates me. No matter how much I tell myself that's the way it is, it still gets to me.

Tsutomu: Well, **I understand your feelings**.

John: Actually, I'm feeling rather good.

Tsutomu: Good. Anything special happen?

John: We got a dog.

Tsutomu: Where did you buy it?

John: Didn't buy it.

Tsutomu: Did someone give it to you?

John: No. No one gave it to us.

Tsutomu: Did you find a stray puppy on the street?

John: No again. **One more guess.**

Tsutomu: I'm not good at guessing. I give up.

約翰兩年前和妻子從美國來到日本，任教於名古屋的某私立大學英語系。努是約翰的同事，教的是中世紀英國文學史。兩人年紀都約四十出頭，彼此相當投緣。某天，結束了漫長的教務會議之後，兩人在努的研究室裡休息、喝咖啡。約翰提到他最近要來一隻小狗，兩人的話題於是從狗的血統一路聊到了人類的混血兒……

約　翰：啊，真高興會議終於結束了，我累得跟狗一樣。《dog-tired 累極了》

努　　：的確是，可是我們要討論的正事就是那麼多。

約　翰：如果是教育方面的事，我不會那麼在意，不過在我看來，大部分都好像是行政上的瑣事。

努　　：約翰，都到這個地步了，你一定知道這是躲不掉的。

約　翰：話是這樣講沒錯，但是我就是很受不了。《It gets to me. = It irritates me.》

努　　：很受不了？

約　翰：是啊，讓我很不耐煩。不管我怎樣告訴我自己事情就是這樣，我還是很受不了。

努　　：嗯，我了解你的感受。

約　翰：其實，我現在覺得蠻高興的。

努　　：那很好啊。是遇到什麼特別的事情嗎？

約　翰：我們養了一隻狗。

努　　：你們去哪裡買的？

約　翰：不是買來的。

努　　：是別人給的嗎？

約　翰：不對，不是別人給的。

努　　：是在路上撿到流浪的小狗嗎？

約　翰：還是不對，再猜猜看。

努　　：我不是很會猜，我放棄。

John: We went to a place that takes stray dogs or dogs that people want to get rid of. If no one takes them within a certain time they are given over to the pound and killed. So, we sort of saved a life.

Tsutomu: Very kind. What kind of dog is it?

John: I really don't know. It's a mongrel.

Tsutomu: I'm sure it's nice. We have a dog too, you know. But my wife is very fussy. She insisted on a purebred.

John: What kind?

Tsutomu: A Dalmatian.

John: Great dog. They're smart and just the right size.

Tsutomu: She's quite clever. But she's been ill twice, and vets are just not cheap.

John: Well, you know, mongrels are hardy. Rarely sick. That's one reason I like them. **They** really **make much more sense**. But in both Japanese and English there's an implicit value judgment in those words, *pure* and *mongrel*.

Tsutomu: You're right. My wife spent $50,000 to get a dog that's cost us almost $100,000. But she's happy. So I'm happy.

John: Nuances can be expensive. You pay for the nice nuance of *pure* and I get a bright, peppy mongrel, part Shepherd and part Akita, free. You know, he was housebroken within only one week. So I'm all for mongrels.

Tsutomu: I guess you know many Japanese are status conscious.

John: So are many Westerners. When it comes to dogs, it's not so crucial. I am bothered, though, by the way Japanese call children when one parent is not Japanese. *International marriage* is O.K.; *mixed marriage*, I don't like so much. But what really gets to me is when they call the children *half*.

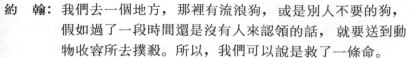

約　翰： 我們去一個地方， 那裡有流浪狗， 或是別人不要的狗，
假如過了一段時間還是沒有人來認領的話， 就要送到動
物收容所去撲殺。 所以， 我們可以說是救了一條命。

努　　： 真好心， 是什麼品種的狗？

約　翰： 我真的不知道耶， 是隻雜種狗。《mongrel = mutt 雜種狗》

努　　： 一定是不錯的狗。 我們也有一隻狗， 可是我老婆很挑剔，
堅持要養純種的狗。

約　翰： 是哪一種？

努　　： 大麥町。

約　翰： 好狗。 這種狗很聰明， 大小也剛好。

努　　： 是很機靈沒錯， 可是生過兩次病， 看獸醫花掉不少錢。

約　翰： 是喔， 可是雜種狗就很強健， 很少生病， 這是我喜歡雜
種狗的原因之一， 養雜種狗比較合理。 不過不管是日文
還是英文， 對於純種和雜種這兩個字， 都隱含價值判斷
的成分。

努　　： 有道理， 我太太花了五萬元買了一隻狗， 這隻狗後來又
花了我們將近十萬元。 不過她覺得很開心， 所以我也覺
得蠻開心的。

約　翰： 細微差異的代價是昂貴的。 你出錢只為了買一隻血統純
正的純種狗， 而我領養了一隻聰明、 活潑的雜種狗， 是
牧羊犬和秋田犬的混種， 一毛錢都不用。 你知道嗎？ 只
過了一個禮拜， 牠的衛生習慣就很好了， 所以我最喜歡
雜種狗了。

努　　： 我想你也知道， 很多日本人社會階級意識都很強。

約　翰： 很多西方人也是一樣。 講到狗的話， 還不是那麼重要，
可是有些小孩的父母只有一方是日本人， 我只要聽到其
他日本人對他們的稱呼， 就有點火大。 說是跨國婚姻還
沒什麼關係， 可是說成是異族通婚我就不是那麼贊成了，
尤其令我受不了的是聽到有人叫那些小孩「半日本人」。

6

Tsutomu: Oh. Is that bad?

John: I suppose Japanese don't mean anything negative. But to me it sounds like the child is only half-human. Maybe I'm wrong but it almost seems as if it's a way to exclude such kids from normal society.

Tsutomu: I've never thought about it. Maybe you're right. But I don't think that's the intention.

John: The intention is one thing. The effect is another.

Tsutomu: What would you call such a child?

John: We'd just say Eurasian. Or Japanese-American. Or Asian-American. You certainly could not say *half* in English; it wouldn't make sense, and some people might resent it.

Tsutomu: Anyway, you make sense. And probably you are more than half-right.

John: Glad you think so. Look at the time. Time to get back home. You know, evenings, it's my turn to walk the dog.

關鍵句

It gets to me.	讓我很不耐煩。／我很受不了。
I understand your feelings.	我了解你的感受。
One more guess.	再猜一次。／再猜猜看。
They make (much more) sense.	這樣（比較）有道理。

努　　：啊，這種稱呼很不好嗎？

約　翰：我想日本人沒有什麼歧視的意思，不過我聽起來就像這小孩只是一半的人，也許我是錯的，不過這幾乎就像是把這種小孩排擠到正常社會之外。

努　　：我從來沒有想過這個問題，也許你說得對，不過我想大家沒有這個意思。

約　翰：有沒有這個意思是一回事，造成的影響又是一回事。

努　　：那你會怎樣稱呼這種小孩呢？

約　翰：我們可能只會說是歐亞混血兒，或是日裔美國人、亞裔美國人。英文絕對不會說是「半人」，這樣沒有道理嘛，有些人聽了也會很生氣。

努　　：不管怎樣，你說的都有道理，而且或許你說的是對的。

約　翰：很高興你也這麼想。看看時間，也該是回家的時候了，傍晚輪到我去溜狗了。

# 7 日出之國的遊戲規則
DOES THE SUN RISE BY DIFFERENT RULES?

Suzanna: Have you read *The Rising Sun* by Michael Crichton?

Kathy: I haven't even seen the movie.

Suzanna: Even though Sean Connery's in it?

Kathy: I admit I like him. And you, have you read the book?

Suzanna: No, that's why I asked. But I have seen the movie.

Kathy: Like it?

Suzanna: Yes, I did, though it's been picketed in some cities.

Kathy: So I've heard. Some Japanese-Americans think it gives a distorted and biased image of Japanese.

Suzanna: But you know who wrote the music for the movie?

Kathy: I have no idea.

Suzanna: Toru Takemitsu, a real famous Japanese composer. Even so, Connery felt obliged to make a statement.

Kathy: What did he say?

Suzanna: Well, he said that he could understand some people finding it offensive but, after all, isn't the corruption at the top level of Japanese business and government pretty scandalous?

Kathy: I suppose it is. But corruption in the States and, say, Italy, sure gives Japan a run for its money.

Suzanna: You know, when I went to school, there were no movies about Japan or scenes at sushi bars. Now Japan has become part of our vocabulary and all these trade problems have become a daily concern.

蘇珊娜（29歲）和凱希（26歲）都是紐約某藥廠的藥品研究員，兩人最近一起請了兩個星期的假到日本旅行。第一個星期過去了，開始想念西式食物的兩個人來到東京六本木的一家法國餐廳用餐。喝著飯後酒，蘇珊娜聊起她之前看過的一部極富爭議性的電影《旭日東昇》，話題不知不覺就轉到日本的非關稅障礙。就連這兩個對日本有好感的外國人，也對日本的作法有些不以為然……

蘇珊娜：妳讀過麥可・克萊頓寫的《旭日東昇》嗎？

凱　希：我連電影版都沒看過。

蘇珊娜：裡面有史恩・康納萊耶，妳沒看過嗎？

凱　希：我是很喜歡他沒錯。那妳呢，有讀過這本書嗎？

蘇珊娜：也沒有，所以我才會問妳啊，不過我看過電影。

凱　希：好看嗎？

蘇珊娜：很好看，不過這部電影遭到某些城市的抗議。

凱　希：我也聽說了，有些日裔美國人覺得這部電影有所偏差，扭曲了日本人的形象。

蘇珊娜：不過妳知道這部電影的配樂是誰寫的嗎？

凱　希：不知道。

蘇珊娜：是武滿徹，他是日本相當有名的作曲家。不過儘管如此，史恩・康納萊還是覺得有必要提出聲明。

凱　希：他說了什麼？

蘇珊娜：嗯，他說他可以理解有些人會覺得很不高興，不過再怎麼說，日本政商高層的貪污腐敗情況不是聲名狼藉的嗎？

凱　希：我想是這樣子沒錯，不過像是美國，還有義大利等國的腐敗情形，不是和日本不相上下嗎？《give ～ a run for its money 與～勢均力敵》

蘇珊娜：在我的學生時代，並沒有什麼和日本有關的電影，也看不到壽司店。可是現在，日本已經成了我們常用辭彙的一部分，貿易問題也是大家日常生活關心的焦點。

Kathy: And **who knows who's at fault**? Probably both sides are. I have a friend in Tokyo—I'll be seeing him next week—who works for the Danish Agricultural Board and he's told me some funny stories.

Suzanna: Like what?

Kathy: Like Japanese dairy companies can buy as much cheese as they want from Denmark, and that cheese just zips through customs. But when the cheese is imported to be sold as Danish cheese, **it's a different ball game**. There are countless regulations and labels and what he calls non-tariff barriers that **are a real pain in the neck**.

Suzanna: On the other hand, I have an American friend I'm seeing tomorrow, and he also has some funny stories. He's a headhunter, though he insists you call it executive search, and he finds Japanese executives for foreign companies in Japan. According to him, some American companies are just not willing to make the kind of commitment that you've got to make to do business here. They want to get in without paying their dues.

Kathy: **That may be.** But I'll bet you those dues are pretty damned high. That's what people mean when they say Japan plays with rules that are just out of this world, out of our world anyway.

Suzanna: I guess so. But if the Japanese play by our rules when they sell in the States, is it crazy to suggest that we play by their rules when we want to sell here?

Kathy: Suzanna, **that sounds plausible**. But aren't you forgetting something? Their rules aren't fair. They're biased, biased in favor of Japanese companies.

Suzanna: Biased. Schmiased.* After all, why should American companies be babied?

Kathy: I thought you liked the movie?

凱　希：誰知道是誰對誰錯？可能兩邊都有錯吧。我有一個朋友在東京，我下禮拜要去找他，他在丹麥農業局上班，他跟我說了一些很荒謬的事情。

蘇珊娜：什麼事情？

凱　希：像是日本乳製品製造公司向丹麥買起司，想買多少就買多少，很快就可以通過海關。可是一旦這些起司要引進日本來，當成丹麥的起司來賣的話，又是另外一回事了。會有數不清的規定、標籤，還有那些他口中的非關稅壁壘，讓人相當頭痛。

蘇珊娜：另一方面，我有一個美國的朋友，我明天要去看他，他也說了一些荒唐的事情。他的工作是物色人才並進行挖角，替日本的一些外商公司挖掘日籍高階幹部，不過他堅持要我們稱他為executive search。根據他的說法，到日本來做生意，要做出一些約定，有些美商公司就是不肯配合，他們想進入日本市場，卻不想付出任何的代價。

凱　希：是有這個可能，不過我敢跟妳打賭，那些金額一定高得嚇死人。大家常說日本人的遊戲規則簡直不是一般人所能接受的，就是這個意思，真的不是我們能接受的。

蘇珊娜：我想是吧。不過如果日本的商品賣到美國來，他們遵守我們的遊戲規則，那我們想把東西賣到日本，就要遵守他們的規則，這有什麼不對？

凱　希：蘇珊娜，妳說的聽起來似乎很合理，不過妳難道忘了？日本原本的規則就不公平了，規則有所偏頗，偏袒日本的公司。

蘇珊娜：管它偏頗不偏頗的，畢竟，為什麼美商公司要受特別的禮遇呢？

凱　希：你不是喜歡這部電影嗎？

7

Suzanna: I did but mainly because I like Sean Connery. Besides, it's a movie. Who in her right mind imagines movies are realistic?

Kathy: **You've said a mouthful.** Say, don't you think we should refresh our drinks?

Suzanna: Rather than do that, why don't we do a little bar-hopping and get a drink somewhere else?

Kathy: **Couldn't agree more.**

關鍵句

Who knows who's at fault?	誰知道是誰對誰錯?
It's a different ball game.	這又是另外一回事了。/ 這是兩碼子事。
~ is [are] a real pain in the neck.	~實在令人頭痛。
That may be.	有(這個)可能。
That [It] sounds plausible.	(這)聽起來似乎很有道理。
You've said a mouthful.	說得好。/ 你說得真是一針見血。
Couldn't agree more.	非常贊成。

蘇珊娜： 我是喜歡這部電影啊，不過主要是因為史恩‧康納萊的
關係。還有，這只是電影嘛，有誰會真的以為電影就是
現實生活？

凱　希： 說得好，對了，我們要不要再叫別的東西喝喝？

蘇珊娜： 倒不如我們換個地方，到其他酒吧去喝一杯吧？

凱　希： 我舉雙手贊成。

○ TIPS FOR EFFECTIVE COMMUNICATION ○

▶ Biased. Schmiased. schmiased是為了押韻而故意模仿
biased所造的字，本身並沒有意思。硬要翻譯的話，大概會是
「管它是偏頗不偏頗的，反正這樣做就是不對」，通常出現在對
方強詞奪理時，回以「說那些是沒有用的」來封住對方的口。
造字原則首先是將該字第一個母音之前的子音拿掉（以母音開
頭的字則維持不變），然後在字首加上Schm，不過例外的情形
也不少，即使是native speaker也不是很清楚，全憑個人感覺在
使用。

8 暧昧的美德
CRYSTAL CLEAR ANSWERS AREN'T ALWAYS THE BEST

George: **It just amazes me** how those old guys still keep at it and how good they are.

Mat: Well, you know that judo here isn't just throwing people to the floor. Spirit, it's the spirit that's the name of the game.

George: I'm beginning to understand that. At first, though, **it was beyond me**. I thought knocking the guy down was the point but **I'm beginning to see the light**.

Mat: George, **you're a quick learner**. **No doubt about it.**

George: Sometimes I have my doubts but I'm going to get my black belt even if it kills me.

Mat: It's when you don't want the belt that you'll get it without killing yourself, that's Zen.*

George: Are you on a Zen kick? I know some Americans who are into Zen but I'll be damned if I know any Japanese who are.*

Mat: Maybe the Japanese who are into Zen aren't into Americans.

George: Look. You've been here much longer than I've been here. So I want to ask.

Mat: Ask. Go ahead.

George: Right. I'm going to ask.

Mat: Right on.

> 馬特（25歲）和喬治（23歲）是兩個開朗的美國人，在東京同一所柔道館學柔道，平日各自在英語補習班教書。馬特來日本已經兩年了，喬治只有半年。這天練習完後，兩人一同搭地下鐵回家。在車廂中，喬治問馬特：「聽說日本人是不說No的，這句話是真的嗎？」馬特回答：「日本人是Yes和No都不會說的民族。」喬治聽得糊裡糊塗，說什麼都要問個清楚……

喬　治： 這些老先生的功夫保持的這麼好，還這麼厲害，真讓人驚訝。

馬　特： 是啊，你也知道，在這裡，柔道不是只要把別人摔到地上就好了，精神，柔道的精神才是最重要的。《the name of the game 最重要的事》

喬　治： 我也漸漸了解到這一點了。可是一開始的時候，我完全無法理解，我以為把對方擊倒才是重點，現在我才慢慢領悟。

馬　特： 你學得很快啊，喬治，這一點是無庸置疑的。

喬　治： 有時候我質疑自己的能力。雖然很辛苦，不過我打算拿黑帶。

馬　特： 只有在你不求黑帶的時候才能輕鬆拿到黑帶，這就是禪的境界。

喬　治： 你對禪也很熱中嗎？我認識一些對禪很熱中的美國人，不過壓根兒就不曉得有這樣的日本人。《be on a ～ kick 熱中於～ / be into ～熱中於～》

馬　特： 可能是對禪很熱中的日本人對美國人不感興趣吧。

喬　治： 對了，你比我在這兒待得還久些，所以有個問題想問你。

馬　特： 問啊，請說。

喬　治： 好，那我要問囉。

馬　特： 說吧。《Right on. = Keep going. 繼續》

George: People always say—why, not too long ago Clinton said— that Japanese don't give a straight yes or no. Now, is that really true?

Mat: Well, I don't know.

George: What kind of an answer is that? Is *that* a nice crystal clear yes or no?* It sure isn't.

Mat: So what you want is a crystal clear yes or no? Right?

George: Right. That's what I want.

Mat: But before I do that, let me ask you: are you perfectly happy with your life?

George: Well, yes and no.

Mat: Well, well, well. What kind of an answer is that? Is that a crystal clear yes or no?

George: Wait a minute. **Just hold your horses.** Your question isn't the kind of question with only a yes or no answer.

Mat: So you think that some questions don't have only yes or no answers?

George: Well, I guess that's right.

Mat: You guess?

George: Well, that's what I think.

Mat: That's what you think?

George: Yeah. That's what I think. **Do you want to make something of it?**

Mat: What I want to make out is if your answer means yes or no or something else.

George: O.K. O.K. **If you push me against the wall:** some questions do have a yes/no answer and some don't. O.K.? Happy?

Mat: Look. Don't get your hackles up. Remember that you were the one who started with these questions.

喬　治：大家都說，像不久前柯林頓總統就說過，日本人都不以
　　　　一個肯定的是或不是來回答問題，想問你是不是真有此
　　　　事？《why＝say 像是……，你看嘛……》

馬　特：嗯，我也不清楚。

喬　治：這是哪門子的回答啊？這是清楚明白的回答嗎？絕對不
　　　　是吧。

馬　特：所以你要的答案是百分之百的肯定或是否定是嗎？

喬　治：沒錯，我要這種答案。

馬　特：不過在我回答以前，我就要先問你啦，你對你的生活十
　　　　分滿意嗎？

喬　治：這個嘛，可以說滿意，也可以說不滿意。

馬　特：這就對啦，你這又是哪門子的回答？是完全滿意還是完
　　　　全不滿意？

喬　治：等一下，稍安勿躁！你的問題不是那種只要回答是或不
　　　　是的問題。

馬　特：所以你是認為有些問題不是只有是或不是的回答囉？

喬　治：嗯，我想是這樣沒錯。

馬　特：你想是這樣？

喬　治：嗯，這是我的想法。

馬　特：這是你的想法？

喬　治：對啊，這就是我的想法，你是想挑我的語病是不是？

馬　特：我只是想弄清楚你的答案代表是還是不是，還是有其他
　　　　的可能。

喬　治：好吧，好吧，如果你硬要這樣逼我的話，我只能說有些
　　　　問題的確可以回答是或不是，不過有些問題就不行，這
　　　　樣可以了嗎？滿意了吧？

馬　特：喂，不要激動，別忘了，是你先問我的喲。

George: Well, maybe I started with questions but I'm sure not getting any answers.

Mat: We now both agree that for some questions yes and no **are no-no's**. And I guess **the bottom line is** that Japanese aren't comfortable with black-and-whites or yes-and-no's. But **it isn't quite that simple**.

George: It is simple; **don't make it complicated**.

Mat: But there're a lot of questions to which we don't answer yes/no; same for the Japanese; trouble is they're not the same questions.

George: I didn't have to ask you to find that out. You like to give lectures, don't you?

Mat: Well, **I wouldn't put it that way**.*

George: Fine. Just how *would* you put it?

Mat: I'm just trying to explain how things seem to me.

George: Isn't there a simpler way to explain something so simple?

Mat: Look. If you think what I'm saying is so simple and if you already know what I'm trying to explain, why did you ask me to begin with?

George: I don't know. I really don't know. I guess I expected a simple yes/no answer.

喬　治：好吧，問題也許是我起頭的，不過看起來我根本沒有得
　　　　到答案。

馬　特：現在我們都同意，有些問題的答案絕對不可能只有單純
　　　　的是或不是。而且我猜根本的原因在於，日本人對於黑
　　　　白分明、非是即非的答案會覺得不自在，但也不是只有
　　　　這麼單純而已。《no-no('s) 不能被接受的事》

喬　治：很單純啦，不要複雜化了。

馬　特：可是有很多問題我們美國人不會回答是或不是；日本人
　　　　也一樣；麻煩就在於這些問題不一樣。

喬　治：我又不是要問你這個，你很喜歡說教，不是嗎?

馬　特：嗯，我不會這樣說（我自己）。

喬　治：沒關係，那你會怎樣說?

馬　特：我剛才只是解釋有些事情在我看來是怎麼一回事而已。

喬　治：這麼簡單的事，難道沒有其他更簡單的方法可以解釋嗎?

馬　特：聽著，如果你覺得我說的很簡單，而且你已經知道我想
　　　　要解釋的是什麼了，那你一開始幹嘛還要問我?

喬　治：我不知道，我真的不知道，我想我只是想聽到很簡單的
　　　　是或不是的回答。

8

It just amazes me ～.	～真是讓我驚訝。
It was beyond me [my understanding].	超出我的理解範圍之外。
I'm beginning to see the light.	我慢慢了解事情的真理。
You're a quick learner.	你學得很快。
No doubt about it.	毫無疑問。／無庸置疑。
(Just) hold your horses.	不要衝動。／別發火。／別急。
Do you want to make something of it?	你是想要找碴，拿～大作文章嗎？
If you push me against the wall.	如果真的非～不可的話。
It's a no-no. ／ They are no-no's.	絕對不可以。／絕對不准。
The bottom line is (that) ～.	根本的原因在於～。／最後的結論是～。
It isn't (quite) that simple.	事情不是這麼簡單。／事情沒有那麼單純。
Don't make it complicated.	不要(把事情)複雜化了。
I wouldn't put it that way.	我不會這樣解釋。／我不會這麼說。

○ TIPS FOR EFFECTIVE COMMUNICATION ○

▶It's when you don't want the belt that you'll get it without killing yourself, that's Zen. 「只有在你不求黑帶的時候才能輕鬆拿到黑帶，這就是禪的境界」 刻意追求反而得不到，往往在你捨棄雜念，一心修煉時，成功才來敲門。看來，馬特對於禪的基本精神：「去私、定心、無我而萬事始成」，似乎有一番領悟。

▶I'll be damned if I know any Japanese who are. 「我壓根兒就不曉得有這樣的日本人」 I'll be damned if ～是「（if後頭的內容）絕對不可能，會有（if後頭的內容）才怪」的俚俗說法。damn的意思是「該死！」，屬於低俗的俚語，使用時須多加注意。例如："I'll be damned if it's true."（那件事會是真的才怪！）／"Damn it."（該死！）／"Damn you!"（去你的！）／"Damn the rain."（討厭的雨！）。

▶Is *that* a nice crystal clear yes or no? 「這是清楚明白的回答嗎？」 用nice強調crystal clear，語氣中略帶諷刺。crystal是水晶，crystal clear是「像水晶一樣清澈，非常清楚」的形容詞，為常見的說法。

▶I wouldn't put it that way. 「我不會這樣說（我自己）」 I wouldn't ～「如果是我的話，我不會～」，put it that way「那樣說／認為」，會話中經常出現。例如："I still don't understand your point."（我還是不懂你的意思）"Then, let's put it this way."（那這樣說好了……）。

9 日本食物用英文怎麼說?
HOW TO TALK ABOUT JAPANESE FOOD

Greg: Ah, this is great. *Kabuto-ni*, I love it, Noriko.

Noriko: I'm glad you love it. And I'm going to really take advantage of you tonight.

Greg: Interesting. Interesting. And just how are you going to take advantage of me?

Noriko: Well, you're not the only non–Japanese* I have to entertain. But most of them don't know what *fugu nabe* is. So I'm going to run through a list and I want you to tell me how I would explain these things to a person who knows no Japanese at all.

Greg: Oh my God.* Just when I was beginning to enjoy myself.

Noriko: First: *kabuto-ni*.

Greg: Gently-boiled large fish-head. Instead of wine you use sake *mirin*—which is sweetened sake, and soy sauce with a stock from bonito flakes and *kombu* seaweed.

Noriko: And *fugu*?

Greg: Blowfish. But nobody eats blowfish. So you have to say *fugu is* blowfish, a fish with big spines and with a poison so deadly that you're certain to die if you eat it. And then, just as your guest is getting worried, you tell him that licensed specialists remove the poison and that it's a seasonal delicacy.

葛瑞格（47歲）是美國一家食品大廠的廣告部主任，被分派到日本分公司已經十年了。典子（39歲）是廣告公司的營業課課長，和葛瑞格因公務而結識，兩人是好朋友。

這天，典子招待葛瑞格到東京淺草的一家壽司店談公事，典子順便請教好友葛瑞格該如何向外國人介紹日本的食物。可能是問題太多了，葛瑞格到最後似乎有些混……

葛瑞格： 啊，這個好，我最喜歡吃*kabuto-ni*（譯者按：日文「醬燒魚頭」之意）了，典子。

典　子： 喜歡吃就好，那我今天晚上就要好好的利用你了。

葛瑞格： 有趣，真有趣，那不知道妳是要怎樣利用我？

典　子： 嗯，我要款待的外國人不是只有你一個，不過他們大多數的人都不知道*fugu nabe*（譯者按：日文「河豚火鍋」之意）是什麼，所以我要瀏覽一下菜單，然後想請你告訴我，如果要跟完全不懂日文的人解釋的話，這些東西要怎麼說。

葛瑞格： 喔，天啊，我才剛要好好品嚐一下呢。

典　子： 第一道是*kabuto-ni*。

葛瑞格： 就是文火煮熟的大魚頭，不是用葡萄酒，而是用清酒、味醂——就是加了甜味的清酒、醬油，然後再加上柴魚片及海帶熬成的高湯來燉煮。

典　子： 那*fugu*呢？

葛瑞格： 河豚，不過（在美國）沒有人吃河豚，所以妳要跟客人說*fugu*就是河豚，是一種很多刺的有毒魚類，毒性很強，只要吃了就會死掉。然後就在客人都很擔心的時候，再告訴他們，有執照的專門調理人員會把毒素都弄掉，還要跟他們說這是特定季節才吃得到的佳餚。

Noriko: *Nabe-ryori.*

Greg: *Nabe. Nabe.* It's boiling ingredients in a cast-iron or earthen-ware vessel but instead of a meat base, the base is some bonito flakes and seaweed; then fish or chicken and vegetables are added. Sometimes it's like a stew.

Noriko: Talk more slowly. **I'm taking notes.**

Greg: Why didn't you bring a tape recorder?

Noriko: Because I know you would hate that.

Greg: **Quite right.** I'd throw the recorder in the *nabe*!

Noriko: So I didn't bring it. Tofu.

Greg: **That's getting easier** because more people abroad know what it is even if they're not eating it. Bean curd. A high-protein form of bean curd, usually white, and cut into cubes. You usually season it because tofu's taste is rather bland.

Noriko: *Natto.*

Greg: It's rotten beans—but don't say that. Just say it's fermented beans, eaten by *ninja*, and that it has a powerful smell like some strong Danish cheeses and is an acquired taste.*

Noriko: An acquired taste?

Greg: Yes. **That's an elegant way of saying that** most people don't like it the first time they try it. Caviar is also an acquired taste.

Noriko: *Miso-shiru.*

Greg: This isn't much of a dialogue. You just say one word and I have to give you a long explanation. **Definitely not fair.**

Noriko: Right. This is not-fair night. *Miso-shiru.*

Greg: **You are persistent.** Miso is bean paste, a Japanese staple

典　子： *Nabe*料理。（譯者按：日文「火鍋」之意）

葛瑞格： *Nabe*，嗯，*nabe*就是將食材放在鐵鍋或是陶鍋中滾煮，不用肉類做鍋底，而是用柴魚片和海帶做鍋底，然後再加魚肉或雞肉，還有青菜，有時候看起來像是一鍋燉湯。

典　子： 講慢一點，我在做筆記。《take notes 做筆記》

葛瑞格： 妳為什麼不拿錄音機？

典　子： 因為我知道你討厭錄音機。

葛瑞格： 沒錯，我會把錄音機丟到*nabe*裡面！

典　子： 所以我才沒帶啊！豆腐呢？

葛瑞格： 這個更容易了，因為比較多外國人知道這是什麼，所以就算他們沒有吃過也知道。妳就直接說bean curd就好了。有豐富的蛋白質，通常是白色的，切成方形，因為沒什麼味道，所以通常都會加調味料。《cut into cubes 切成方形 / season〔動詞〕調味，加調味料》

典　子： *Natto*。（譯者按：日文「納豆」之意）

葛瑞格： 就是腐爛的豆子，不過不要這樣說，只要說是發酵過的豆子就好了，是忍者在吃的，而且有一種很重的味道，有點像丹麥某些味道很重的起司，這種味道要後天學過才會喜歡吃。

典　子： 要後天學過才喜歡吃的味道？

葛瑞格： 對，這樣的說法比較風雅，指大部分的人第一次吃的時候都不喜歡的味道，像魚子醬也是一種吃過才會喜歡的味道。

典　子： *Miso-shiru*。（譯者按：日文「味噌湯」之意）

葛瑞格： 真不像是在對話，妳只要說一個字，我就要跟你解釋一長串，真不公平。

典　子： 沒錯，今天晚上就是不公平。*Miso-shiru*。

葛瑞格： 妳很堅持耶。*Miso*就是豆醬，是日本人的主食，每一餐

After every Japanese meal, you get miso-soup called *miso-shiru* in a small lacquered wooden bowl and though it's a soup, you get it with chopsticks. What you do is lift the bowl close to your mouth and as you suck up the soup, you use the chopsticks to scoop the seaweed or chopped up leeks or tiny mushrooms that are in the soup into your mouth.

Noriko: You're talking too fast. **I can't get all this down.** And it's too complicated.

Greg: **That's not my fault.** Fact is, consuming miso-soup is a complicated process.

Noriko: *Shabu-shabu*.

Greg: You take some expensive beef and slice it real thin. Then you take a fancy bronze-like pot which has a large, very short tube running through the middle. You fill it up with water and then, you pick up a slice of beef with your chopsticks and dip it in the boiling water until it's done; then you dip that beef into one of several sauces. Usually you got a sesame sauce and a tart sauce. Besides the meat, you throw in vegetables and finally, you throw noodles in the broth.

Noriko: Very good. Very good. *Wasabi*.

Greg: *Wasabi*. Schmasabi. **Enough is enough.** Just get us some more beer. I insist you have some beer too.

Noriko: But **I get stewed so easily** you know.

Greg: I know. That's the point.*

Noriko: Soon I won't know what I'm doing.

Greg: That's why I want you to drink some more so it'll be my turn to take advantage of you!

飯後都會有味噌湯,就是 *miso-shiru*,用漆器的木碗裝著。雖然是湯,不過會給一雙筷子,吃法就是把碗端到嘴邊,然後喝湯的時候, 就用筷子去把湯裡面的海帶、 蔥花或是小蘑菇撈到嘴裡。《tiny mushroom 小蘑菇》

典　子:你講得太快了,我沒有辦法全部寫下來,太複雜了。

葛瑞格:不是我的錯, 事實上, 喝味噌湯的步驟本來就很複雜。

典　子:*Shabu-shabu*。(譯者按:日文「涮涮鍋」之意)
葛瑞格:就是把高價的牛肉切成很薄很薄, 然後用高級的青銅之類的鍋子, 鍋子中間會有很粗很短的管狀物體, 把水放滿, 然後用筷子夾起一片牛肉,泡到滾湯裡面, 熟了以後就拿出來沾醬, 通常會有芝麻醬和酸桔醬。 除了肉之外, 也要把青菜放進去,最後再把麵放到高湯裡面。《broth = stock》。

典　子:講得好,講得好。*Wasabi*。(譯者按:日文「芥末」之意)
葛瑞格:*Wasabi*,什麼 *wasabi*,真的不要再說了,再多拿一點啤酒來吧,我覺得妳也要多喝一點啤酒。《*Wasabi*. Schmasabi. 請參照第45頁的TIPS FOR EFFECTIVE COMMUNICATION》
典　子:不過你也知道, 我很容易醉的。《get stewed = get drunk》
葛瑞格:我知道, 這才是重點啊。
典　子:我會一下子就不知道自己在做什麼了耶。
葛瑞格:所以我才要妳多喝啊,這樣才能換我利用妳啊!

"Pardon?"恐懼症

　　對自己的英語程度沒有信心的人，通常只要聽到對方說"Pardon?"，就以為自己說錯話，羞得不敢開口。其實沒什麼好怕的，不管是"Pardon?"還是"I beg your pardon?"，不過是對方沒聽清楚，而不見得是你說錯了話。下次再遇到相同情形時，記得不要慌張，清楚地重複之前所說的話，不要被"Pardon?"給嚇到了，這是可以自我訓練的。

(((關鍵句)))

I'm taking notes.	我在做筆記。
(That's) quite right.	對極了。/完全正確。
That's getting easier.	這個簡單多了。/這個越來越容易了。
That's an elegant way of saying that ~.	這樣說～比較風雅。
Definitely not fair.	真的很不公平。
You are persistent.	你很堅持。/你很頑固。
I can't get all this down.	我沒有辦法全部記〔寫〕下來。
That's not my fault.	這不是我的錯。
Enough is enough.	真的夠了。
I get stewed (so easily).	我（很容易就）喝醉了。

○ TIPS FOR EFFECTIVE COMMUNICATION ○

▶ **non-Japanese** 這年頭很忌諱「歧視」性的字眼，我們平常以為不帶評價的foreigner，同樣也有類似的感覺，所以有些人喜歡用「非本國人」的形式來稱呼外國人，例如：non-Japanese。另外還有alien的說法，意思是「局外人，和自己無關的人」，是這三個字之中給人感覺最生疏的：alien ＞ foreigner ＞ non-Japanese。

▶ **Oh my God.**「喔，天啊！」 原本是遇到困難時向上帝求助的用語，如今已經成為「喔，不會吧！」、「慘了！」的感嘆詞，和上帝一點關係也沒有。部分人士因為覺得直呼上帝的名諱太不敬，所以換掉God，改成以下的說法："Oh my gosh." "Oh my goodness."。

▶ **an acquired taste**「要後天學過才喜歡吃的味道」 意思是需要一些時間或多接觸才懂得欣賞的味道。像是魚子醬、藍乳酪、海膽等等，由於味道特殊，第一次嘗試的人往往不能接受，多試過幾次之後才嚐得出滋味。這個說法也可以用在人的身上，例如："Sally is an acquired taste."（莎莉是個需要相處才知道她的好的人）。

▶ **That's the point.**「這才是重點啊／那正是我的目的」 point在此是「目的、著眼點」的意思，如果語氣想再強烈一點，可以說"That's the whole point."。

10 賭博? 投資?
GAMBLING VS. INVESTING

Ralph: Look, Michio, I've got some eight million dollars that I don't need right now and that I probably won't have to touch for more than a year. What should I put it in?

Michio: **The safest thing is** a bank time deposit.

Ralph: A time deposit? In a Japanese bank? Low interest rates and high penalties if you pull out before due date are not for me.

Michio: But that's what many people do.

Ralph: **I'm not many people.** What I meant was: what stocks or bonds or mutual funds are a good bet?

Michio: Stocks? You're interested in stocks?

Ralph: Well, I thought I was. But it seems that the smallest amount you can buy here is in units of a thousand. So if I got some blue chips, I wouldn't have much variety in my portfolio. Never put all your eggs in one basket,* you know.

Michio: I suppose the Japanese market isn't geared to individual investors.*

Ralph: **Truer words were never spoken.** * What's even more discouraging is that the PE's are unbelievably high and the yield is abysmally low.

Michio: That's because there's high taxation on dividends.

Ralph: How about some mutual funds?

> 　道夫（42歲）和雷爾夫（45歲）在某次露營活動中結識，雷爾夫是加拿大人，在日本住了將近六年，從事加拿大組合式小木屋的進出口生意，前一陣子景氣好，賺了不少錢。道夫是法國某銀行的投資經紀人，兩人固定每週四約在日比谷的一家印度料理店吃午餐。
>
> 　這天，兩人照常在老地方共進午餐聊天，雷爾夫說他手頭有一筆錢，問道夫該如何投資，問啊問的……

雷爾夫： 道夫啊，我有差不多八百萬元，目前用不到，一年之內可能也都用不到，放哪裡比較好？《some = about》

道　夫： 最安全的方法就是銀行定存了。

雷爾夫： 定存？放在日本的銀行？利息那麼低，而且如果在合約到期日之前就領出來損失可大了，不適合我。《penalty 因解約而伴隨而來的嚴重後果／pull out = withdraw 取款》

道　夫： 不過很多人都是這樣做的啊！

雷爾夫： 我又不是很多人。我的意思是說，有沒有什麼股票、債券或是共同基金之類好投資的？

道　夫： 股票？你對股票有興趣？

雷爾夫： 嗯，應該是吧，不過在這裡好像最少都要買一千股，所以如果我買的是績優股的話，那我的投資組合就沒有多少種類了，不要把雞蛋放在同一個籃子裡，知道吧。
　　《portfolio 有價證券組合清單》

道　夫： 我認為日本的股市不適合個別的投資人。《gear to ~ 使適合 ~，使合乎~》

雷爾夫： 你說得一點也沒錯。更令人失望的就是本益比高得不得了，而獲利率又非常低。《PE = price-earning ratio 本益比》

道　夫： 那是因為股息都要課很多的稅。

雷爾夫： 那共同基金呢？

Michio: Well, there are some but I'm not sure you'd like them.

Ralph: What's the problem?

Michio: First of all, they are all front-load funds, and, even worse, **from what I know**, there are few reliable high performers.

Ralph: So what do we have left?

Michio: Government bonds, money market funds and short-term debentures.

Ralph: What's the risk factor?

Michio: Just about zero. For the best interest with the lowest risk, these three instruments might be your best bet.

Ralph: Well, I suppose so. It's just that you can't make any real money that way and, it's boring.

Michio: Well, if you want some risk and enjoy excitement, **I know just the thing**.

Ralph: **Now you're talking.***

Michio: We'll go to *kyotei*.

Ralph: What's that?

Michio: These are small speed boats; it's like stock car racing but instead of cars, peppy little speed boats and the atmosphere is great!

Ralph: **What**, just what, Michio, **has** *kyotei* **got to do with** investing?

Michio: **I told you.** It's like stock car racing. You pick a boat to win or place.

Ralph: That's gambling. You are talking about gambling.

Michio: Didn't you say you wanted a shot at big winnings? Didn't you say you wanted excitement?

Ralph: Yeah, but **I didn't say anything about** gambling.

Michio: Isn't playing the stock market gambling?

Ralph: No, it's investing.

道　夫：嗯，是有一些，不過我不知道你會不會中意。

雷爾夫：有什麼問題？

道　夫：首先，它們都會先收手續費，更糟的是，就我所知，表現好的基金沒有幾支。

雷爾夫：那還剩下什麼選擇？

道　夫：政府公債、貨幣市場基金，或是短期公司債券。

雷爾夫：有什麼風險嗎？

道　夫：幾乎沒有，利潤最好，風險最低，這三種方法可能是你最好的投資選擇。

雷爾夫：嗯，我想也是。不過這樣就沒辦法獲取很高的利潤，而且很無聊。《real money = large profit 豐厚的利潤》

道　夫：嗯，如果你想要冒險，要享受刺激的話，我知道一樣東西很適合你。《just the thing 合適，符合所需》

雷爾夫：你現在才說到重點。

道　夫：我們可以去玩 *kyotei*（譯者按：日文「賽艇」之意）。

雷爾夫：那是什麼？

道　夫：是一些小型的快艇，就好像在賽車，不過這不是用車子，而是用衝勁十足的小型快艇，氣氛超棒的。《peppy 衝勁十足的，速度快的》

雷爾夫：道夫，等一下，*kyotei* 跟投資到底有什麼關係？

道　夫：剛跟你說啦！就像賽車一樣，你賭其中一輛快艇會獲勝或是進入前三名。《place〔動詞〕得前三名》

雷爾夫：哎，你說的那個是賭博耶！

道　夫：你不是說你想要馬上致富？你不是說你想要刺激的嗎？《shot = chance》

雷爾夫：是啊，不過我根本就沒有說要賭博啊。

道　夫：那你覺得玩股票是不是賭博？

雷爾夫：才不是，那是投資。

Michio: If you buy gold, aren't you gambling?

Ralph: Of course not; I'm investing.

Michio: Don't you buy gold hoping the price goes up?

Ralph: Of course.

Michio: And can you ever be sure the price will go up?

Ralph: Of course not.

Michio: So aren't you gambling that the price of gold will go up?

Ralph: Well, if you put it that way...

Michio: If you buy a stock and the bottom drops out of the market, how do you feel?

Ralph: Awful. Just awful.

Michio: So why not gamble? After all, even if you lose, at least you will have had some fun. Put 80% of your money into a super-*teiki*; then take 20% with you and let's enjoy the boats!

Ralph: O.K. Let's live dangerously.

You pick a boat to win or place.

That's gambling.

道　夫：那如果你買黃金是不是賭博？

雷爾夫：當然不是啊，也是投資。

道　夫：你買黃金是不是希望價格能夠上揚？

雷爾夫：當然啦。

道　夫：那你能確定價格一定會上揚嗎？

雷爾夫：當然沒辦法。

道　夫：所以你是不是在賭金價會上揚？

雷爾夫：嗯，如果你硬要這樣說的話……

道　夫：如果你買了一支股票，後來股價跌到意外的低水平，你有什麼感想？

雷爾夫：很糟，糟透了。

道　夫：那為什麼不去賭博？再怎麼說，就算賭輸了，至少也享受到一點樂趣嘛。你把百分之八十的錢放到super-*teiki*（譯者按：日文「銀行的超級定期儲金」之意），再拿百分之二十的錢，我們好好去賭一賭快艇！

雷爾夫：好吧，就過一下驚險的生活吧！

10

讓我想一想……

　　有些人的英語會話能力其實不錯，就是反應不快，一遇到對方發問，一緊張之下，嘴巴閉得緊緊的，腦子裡只想著怎麼回答，卻不知對方見你不講話，還以為你聽不懂，無形中給人很遜的印象。像這種時候，至少要說Well... / Let's see... / Let me see... / Let me think...，一來讓對方了解你懂他的意思，二來也可以為自己爭取一些思考的時間。

關鍵句

The safest thing is ～.	最安全的做法就是～。
I'm not many people.	我不是一般人。/ 我和許多人不同。
Truer words were never spoken.	說得完全正確。/ 一點兒也沒錯。
From what I know,	就我所知～
I know just the thing.	我知道什麼最合適。
Now you're talking.	這才像話。/ 你這才說到重點。
What has A got to do with B?	A和B到底有什麼關係?
I told you.	早就跟你說過了。
I didn't say anything about ～.	我(根本就)沒有提到～。

○ TIPS FOR EFFECTIVE COMMUNICATION ○

▶ Never put all your eggs in one basket（成語）「不要把雞蛋放在同一個籃子裡」　意思是不要拿所有的財產來孤注一擲。put [have] all one's eggs in [into] one basket是「將所有希望寄託在一件事物上」或是「將全部財產投資在單一事業上」的片語。

▶ individual investor(s)「個別投資人」　就是一般人口中說的「散戶」，反義字是institutional investor（法人投資）。日本股市的成交單位大多是從一千股起跳，顯然是將客戶層鎖定在法人及自營商，加上傳統上認為「股票是碰不得的」的觀念影響，一般而言，日本民眾將錢投資在股票以及債券的人數並不多，不像美國中產階級(average middle class)幾乎人人手中都有持股或是債券。兩國國情不同固然是一項因素，但是一個社會對散戶投資的服務機制是否完善，也扮演了極大的影響。

▶ Truer words were never spoken.「你說得一點也沒錯」　直譯是「不可能有更貼切的說法了」，　相當於What you said is absolutely true.。說法略顯文縐縐，聽來像是格言，適合用在正式場合或是開玩笑時。

▶ Nów you're talking.「你現在才說到重點」　now必須加強語氣才能達到預期的效果，　意思是 "Now you're talking about what I want to hear." (現在你才說出我想聽到的話)，會話中經常使用。

11 約會：兩個幾乎沒有交集的人
DATING: TWO PEOPLE WHO HAVE LITTLE IN COMMON

Andy: You look pretty busy today, Helen.

Helen: Well, I *am* busy but not as busy as I look.

Andy: That's good.

Helen: Looks can be deceiving, you know.

Andy: Well, maybe you only look pretty busy but you certainly do look pretty today.

Helen: Today? Did I hear you stress "today?"

Andy: Come on. You always look good but today your good looks strike me. In fact...

Helen: In fact, what?

Andy: Well, how about having dinner and taking in a movie?

Helen: This is sudden.

Andy: Actually, I've been thinking about asking you out for almost a week.

Helen: Well...

Andy: Tonight. Right after work.

Helen: O.K. Andy. Sounds like a good idea.

Andy: Great. Now for dinner, I know a first-class Szechwan restaurant.

Helen: Szech? What kind of cooking is that?

> 　　安迪（32歲）和海倫（29歲）都在美國波士頓一家保險公司工作，兩人任職於同單位已經一年。某日下午，一直暗戀海倫的安迪決定化心動為行動，邀海倫一同出去。
>
> 　　初步的邀請是成功了，但是兩人對於接下來該去哪間餐廳，該看什麼電影，意見似乎有些不對盤。安迪百般迎合海倫，但是這次約會會成功嗎？

安　迪：海倫，妳今天看起來很忙碌。《pretty = very》

海　倫：嗯，我是很忙，不過沒有看起來那麼忙。

安　迪：好極了。

海　倫：外表是會騙人的，知道吧。

安　迪：喔，可能妳是看起來很忙，不過妳今天看起來真是漂亮。《第二個pretty = beautiful》

海　倫：今天？你是強調只有今天嗎？

安　迪：別這樣，妳每天都很漂亮，不過今天妳的美貌更是讓我的眼睛為之一亮，其實……《strike 打動，給（人）印象》

海　倫：其實什麼？

安　迪：嗯，要一起吃頓晚餐、看場電影嗎？《take in a movie = go to a movie》

海　倫：太突然了。

安　迪：其實我想約妳出去，已經想了快一個禮拜了。《ask (someone) out 邀約（某人）》

海　倫：這樣喔……

安　迪：今天晚上，一下班就去。

海　倫：好啊，安迪，這個主意聽起來不錯。

安　迪：太棒了，晚餐的話，我知道有一家高級的四川料理店。《Szechwan 四川的》

海　倫：四川？是怎樣的料理啊？

11

Andy: It's a Chinese style, rather spicy and delicious.

Helen: Spicy? I don't mind Chinese food but spicy food doesn't agree with me.*

Andy: O.K. Sushi. Japanese food. Nothing spicy and wonderfully healthy.

Helen: Sushi? Not only did I have sushi two days ago, but I'm just a bit tired of this fad for Japanese food.

Andy: **Forget** the Orient. Can you go for Italian, and I don't mean just some pizza.

Helen: I know Italian food is good, but they use so much garlic and **I'm not a** garlic **lover**.

Andy: O.K. O.K. Japanese is out. Chinese is out. Italian is out. You tell me, what *would* you like? McDonald's?

Helen: You don't have to become sarcastic just because I don't share your palate. How about some nice old-fashioned American home cooking?

Andy: You mean meat loaf?

Helen: Well, it doesn't have to be meat loaf but some good simple home cooking is for me tonight.

Andy: Helen, **I have to tell you that** I don't know such a place but if you do, great, let's go.

Helen: **Let's make it** Dinty Moore's.* They have cherry clams steamed in a basket, clam chowder, and three different kinds of draft beer.

Andy: **We're in business.** Now to the movie. There's a sci-fi film that's gotten good reviews, a new French mystery, and a drama about Prague after the Russians left. Now, which would you like?

Helen: **I leave it up to you.**

安　迪：是中國菜的一種，很辣，很好吃。

海　倫：很辣？中國菜是無所謂，不過辛辣的食物不合我的胃口。

安　迪：好吧，那吃壽司好了，日本料理一點都不會辣，也很健康。《wonderfully = very》

海　倫：壽司？別說我前兩天才吃過壽司，而且我對日本食物一時的流行也有點厭煩了。《fad 流行，一時的狂熱》

安　迪：那就不要東方的食物好了，妳喜歡義大利菜嗎？我不是專指披薩而已喔。《go for ～ 喜歡～，贊成～》

海　倫：我知道義大利菜很好吃，不過他們放很多的大蒜，我不喜歡大蒜。

安　迪：好吧，好吧，日本料理出局了，中國菜出局了，義大利菜也出局了，那妳說說看妳要吃什麼？麥當勞嗎？《out = out of the question 不列入考慮的，不可能的》

海　倫：不要因為我喜歡吃的東西和你不一樣就挖苦我嘛。美式古早味家常菜你覺得怎麼樣？《palate 口味，嗜好》

安　迪：妳是說碎肉捲嗎？

海　倫：嗯，也不只有碎肉捲啦，就是一些簡單好吃的家常菜，我今天晚餐很想吃。

安　迪：海倫，我得坦白跟妳說，我不知道這樣的店，假如妳知道的話最好，那我們就一起去吧！

海　倫：那就去Dinty Moore's（波士頓的愛爾蘭餐廳）好了，他們有清蒸蛤蜊、蛤蜊濃湯，還有三種不同的生啤酒。《make it ～決定～ / cherry clam = cherrystone 蛤蜊的一種》

安　迪：就這麼決定了。那電影的話，有一部科幻片的評價不錯，還有一部剛上映的法國懸疑片，另外也有一部作品，是描寫俄軍離開布拉格以後的情形，那不知道妳想看哪一部？《sci-fi = science fiction / reviews 影評》

海　倫：留給你決定。

11

Andy: How about Prague?

Helen: Well, **I'll bet** it's a political film and, frankly, **I'm a bit sick of** politics.

Andy: O.K. O.K. Let's make it the French movie.

Helen: You know I wonder why some people only go for foreign food and foreign movies?

Andy: Helen, why don't you tell me what movie you would like to see. It'll be simpler.

Helen: Isn't there a good Western around?

Andy: A Western? You mean with John Wayne?

Helen: Well, it doesn't have to be John Wayne, but a good Western is what I'm in the mood for tonight.

Andy: A Western it is and I'm sure we can find one. Let's check the papers.

Helen: Let's see... Oh, here's one, *Shane*.

Andy: Haven't you seen that oldie?

Helen: Oh, I've seen it, years ago. I could see it again.

Andy: Well, **to tell you the truth**, Helen, I've seen it too, but I'd rather not see it again. Besides, it's in a movie house that's way out of the way.

Helen: Are you asking me out so you can eat what you want to eat and see what you want to see?

Andy: Of course not, Helen. Of course not. I want the two of us to have a good time.

Helen: Good. That's how I feel too. Look, I have an idea. You agree Dinty Moore's is O.K. So why not forget about the movie and take in a show or a play instead?

Andy: **I'll buy that!*** There's a terrific off-Broadway comedy that I'll bet you'll go for.

安　迪：布拉格那一部可以嗎？

海　倫：啊，我敢打賭那一定是政治片，不過坦白說，我有點討厭政治。

安　迪：好好好，那就看法國片好了。

海　倫：你知道嗎？我就是搞不懂為什麼有些人就一定要吃外國菜、看外國電影？

安　迪：海倫，妳為什麼不直接跟我說妳想看什麼電影，這樣還比較簡單。

海　倫：沒有什麼好看的西部片嗎？

安　迪：西部片？妳是說要有約翰・韋恩演的電影嗎？

海　倫：不一定是要約翰・韋恩演的電影啦，不過我今天晚上很想看一部好看的西部片。

安　迪：那就決定看西部片啦，我們一定能找到想看的，看一下報紙好了。

海　倫：我看看……啊，有一部，「原野奇俠」。

安　迪：妳沒看過那部老片嗎？《oldie 過去風行的電影》

海　倫：喔，好幾年前就看過了，可是我可以再看一遍。

安　迪：嗯，海倫，老實說，我也看過那部片，我不想再看一遍，而且那家電影院很遠又不順路。

海　倫：你邀我出來就是為了吃你想吃的東西、看你想看的電影嗎？

安　迪：當然不是啦，海倫，我是希望我們兩個人能在一起玩得很高興。

海　倫：很好，我也是這麼想。這樣的話，我想到了，你贊成去吃Dinty Moore's 這家店，那電影就不要理它了，可以去看場秀或是戲劇表演什麼的。

安　迪：我贊成！有一部很棒的外百老匯喜劇，我敢說妳一定會喜歡。

11

Helen: What's it about?

Andy: It's about a couple who go on a date and discover that they've nothing in common.

Helen: Andy, **no doubt about it**. With your sense of humor, we got a lot in common.

Andy: Those are the words I want to hear.

關鍵句

Forget ～. / Forget it.	別管～了。/ 算了吧!
I'm not a ～ lover.	我不是～的愛好者。
I have to tell you that ～.	我得跟你說～。
Let's make it ～.	那就決定做（選）～了。
We're in business.	就這麼決定了。/ 準備就緒。
I leave it up to you.	（這個）留給你決定。
I'll bet ～.	我敢說～。/ 我確信～。
I'm (a bit) sick of ～.	我對～（有點）厭煩了。
To tell you the truth,	老實說～
I'll buy that!	我贊成。
No doubt about it.	毫無疑問。/ 沒什麼好懷疑的。

海　倫：內容在講什麼？

安　迪：是說一對男女出去約會，後來發現他們一點交集也沒有。

海　倫：安迪，不用懷疑，你這麼有幽默感，我們兩個有很多共
　　　　同的話題。

安　迪：這才是我想聽的話。

○ TIPS FOR EFFECTIVE COMMUNICATION ○

▶spicy food doesn't agree with me「辛辣的食物不合我的胃
口」　not agree with ～是「不合適～」，大多指食物引起體質
上的不適，例如：過敏等，但也可以用於個人對食物的偏好。

▶Dinty Moore's　位於波士頓的愛爾蘭餐廳。美國移民中有許
多是愛爾蘭人，愛爾蘭食物也算是美國家常菜的一種，尤其是
波士頓，愛爾蘭移民非常多，Dinty Moore's指的就是提供愛爾
蘭菜的典型餐廳。

▶I'll buy that!（俚語）「我贊成！」　這裡的buy指的是「接受
(accept)，同意（意見、說明）」，也可以說成I can agree with that.，
是個經常使用的說法。

12 東京早晨的人潮
PROBLEMS OF THE MORNING RUSH IN TOKYO

Tim: So, what's new?*

Leroy: Nothing's new. I wish there was something new.

Tim: Well, there's always something new.

Leroy: The only thing that's new is that I've given up driving to work. Traffic's so bad, why, by the time I get to the office, I'm exhausted. And it takes me almost two hours.

Tim: That's why I take the train.

Leroy: I suppose the train does make more sense. But it's so crowded. If I exhale deeply I'm worried I won't be able to inhale again.

Tim: Well, you'll be glad to hear that things are looking up, at least on the Yamanote Line.

Leroy: **It's hard to believe.**

Tim: **You've got to give** JR **credit**. They've improved it.

Leroy: And how have they improved it? It's not possible. They can't run any more trains because the scheduling is so tight right now that a train pulls in almost one second after a train pulls out.

Tim: You're right; they're not running more trains.

Leroy: They can't put more cars on a train because of the length of the platforms.

利若伊（35歲）和提姆（37歲）是美國某雜誌社的東京特派員，到
日本已經三年的時間。這天早上，兩人在位於日比谷的事務所喝咖啡，
一邊聊起東京的交通。利若伊抱怨說：「開車通勤太浪費時間，所以才
改搭電車，沒想到電車擠得不像話！」提姆回說：「JR山手線增設了新型
車輛，人潮應該可以得到疏解。」結果被利若伊潑了盆冷水，說那簡直
是反效果，究竟誰說的才對呢？

提　姆：最近好嗎？

利若伊：老樣子，真希望有點新鮮事。

提　姆：天底下到處都有新鮮事啊。

利若伊：唯一的新鮮事就是我不再開車去上班了，交通那麼糟，
等我到了辦公室，都累癱了，而且幾乎都要花上兩個小
時的時間。《traffic 交通 / why = gee / exhausted 筋疲力盡的》

提　姆：所以我才會搭電車。

利若伊：我想，搭電車是比較明智的作法，可是實在是太擠了，
如果我深吐出一口氣，我都怕下一口氣就吸不到了。
《make more sense 比較合理》

提　姆：那你一定很高興聽到情況已經漸漸好轉了，至少山手線
是這樣。

利若伊：真是難以置信。

提　姆：這都是JR的功勞，是他們改善山手線的。

利若伊：那他們是怎麼改善的？不可能啊，他們又不能多加班次，
因為目前的時刻表已經很滿了，一輛電車剛開走，另一
輛電車馬上就進站了。

提　姆：沒錯，他們不是多加班次。

利若伊：他們也不能在電車上加掛車廂啊，月臺的長度有限。《car
車廂》

Tim: Right again. They're not adding cars.

Leroy: So how could they improve things?

Tim: The new cars now hold more people.

Leroy: Hold more people? Why, they hold too many people right now.

Tim: Now there's more space for more people.

Leroy: What did they do? Remove the seats?

Tim: **You're close.** Not only did they remove seats, they added more doors so more people can get in and out easier.

Leroy: **You're kidding.** They took out all the seats?

Tim: Not all, just some. And what they've done is devilishly clever. From the first train until 10:00 A.M., those seats fold up so there's more space and more people can get on.

Leroy: You mean if I want to sit, I can't get on the train until *after* ten?

Tim: And they've added TV monitors so you can watch educational programs, Japanese history, for example.

Leroy: Look. The last thing I want to do in the morning is to be educated. The less I have to look at, the happier I am.

Tim: Of course, not all the cars are the new type. **Chances are** you'll be riding in the old type for quite a while.

Leroy: Thank Goodness!

Tim: Don't be so negative. Don't you think it's a good idea to have made more space?

Leroy: Frankly no. I think it's a lousy idea.

Tim: Leroy, **I don't follow you**.

Leroy: Look. If the people in the train had more space, maybe that's progress. **But that's theory. In practice**, more space means more people will fit in each car; but that does not mean that each

提　姆： 你又說對了，他們也不是加掛車廂。

利若伊： 那他們要怎樣改善呢？

提　姆： 現在的新車廂可以容納更多的人。

利若伊： 容納更多的人？不會吧，他們目前的載客量已經夠多了。

提　姆： 可是現在有更多的空間可以載更多的人。

利若伊： 他們是怎麼辦到的？把座位拆掉嗎？

提　姆： 很接近了。他們不只把座位拆掉，還增加車門，這樣方便讓更多的人上下車。

利若伊： 不會吧!?他們把所有的椅子都拆了？

提　姆： 不是所有的椅子，只有一些。他們的作法實在是太聰明了，從頭班車開始一直到早上十點這段時間，座椅就摺疊起來，這樣就有更多的空間讓更多的人上車。

利若伊： 你是說如果我想要有座位的話，就要等十點以後再去搭車囉？

提　姆： 而且他們還加裝電視螢幕，可以觀看教育節目，比方說日本歷史。

利若伊： 聽好，一大早我最不想做的事就是「受教育」，什麼都不要看最快樂。

提　姆： 當然啦，不是所有的車廂都是新型的，很可能有一段時間你搭到的都是舊型的車廂。

利若伊： 謝天謝地！

提　姆： 別這麼消極嘛，你不覺得多製造一點空間也挺好的嗎？

利若伊： 坦白說，我覺得不好，我覺得這是一個很爛的方法。

提　姆： 利若伊，你這樣講我就不懂了。

利若伊： 你看嘛，如果車廂裡頭的每個人都有更大空間的話，也許算是有改善，不過那只是理論而已。實際上，更多的空間就代表每個車廂會塞進更多的人，而不是每個人的

individual is going to have more space. In fact, probably there will be less space for each person because, without seats, they can squeeze together more. Now we really will be like the proverbial sardines in a can.

Tim: Well, I wonder.

Leroy: You can wonder **until the cows come home**. These great planners, these great engineers who don't look at the way the world really works get my goat.

Tim: But you said you're switching from car to train.

Leroy: After what you've told me, now it's my turn to wonder.

關鍵句

It's hard to believe.	真是不敢相信。
You've got to give ~ credit.	這得歸功於～。／這都是～的功勞。
You're close.	很接近了。／快說中了。
You're kidding.	你在開玩笑吧？　／不會吧？
Chances are ~.	很有可能～。
I don't follow you.	我不懂你在說什麼。
But that's theory.	可是那只是理論而已。
In practice,	實際上～
Until [Till] the cows come home	長時間地／永遠地

空間會變大。事實上，每個人的空間可能反而變小了，因為椅子拿掉以後，大家就可以擠得更緊，那就真的像是俗話說的「擠沙丁魚」了。《That's theory. 那是理論上來說》

提　姆：嗯，是這樣嗎？

利若伊：你慢慢想吧，這些偉大的決策人員、偉大的工程師都閉門造車，真是讓人生氣。《get one's goat 使某人生氣》

提　姆：不過你剛才不是說你不開車，現在改搭電車了。

利若伊：你跟我說了這件事以後，現在換我要好好考慮考慮了。

○ TIPS FOR EFFECTIVE COMMUNICATION ○

▶ So, what's new?　What's new?（句尾語調下降）比How are you?隨興的說法，經常用在會話中。當朋友久未見面，甚或經常見面但一直沒有時間好好聊時，如同字面上的意思「有什麼新鮮事?」，用來詢問對方的近況。有時也作招呼語使用，就像Hi.和Hello.一樣，沒有特別的意思。另一個說法是Anything new?（句尾語調上揚）。

如果沒有什麼「新鮮事」，或是不想和對方多談時，可以用 "Nothing special." 或是 "Not much." 來回答。

13 好人做到底
HOW TO BE A GOOD GUY

Nagao: I've just been given a new responsibility.

Dean: Yeah? What is it?

Nagao: Well, you know that a new person from the Chicago office is coming to work with us.

Dean: Sure, **I've heard about it**. Her name's Joy Cooper but I don't know her at all.

Nagao: Whenever a new person joins our staff, we give a welcoming party and I've been selected as the host, which means I have to pick the place and organize everything.

Dean: **Good luck to you!**

Nagao: Thanks. But I was wondering...

Dean: Wondering what?

Nagao: Look. Even if you don't know Ms. Cooper, you would certainly have a better idea of what she would like than I would.

Dean: **I don't know about that.**

Nagao: I learned an expression from you, "**be a good guy.**" So, be a good guy and help me with this party.

Dean: **Good grief!** Me? Little ole me?

Nagao: You're six feet tall, so you're not little. And you're under forty, so you're not old.

Dean: Alright. You win. What do we do?

Nagao: The date's fixed, two weeks from next Tuesday. So what we have to do is pick the place and decide on the menu.

永雄（33歲）和迪恩（32歲）是美國某洗滌劑製造廠日本大阪分公司的職員，最近從芝加哥有位新同事要調來，同仁們打算為她辦場迎新會，永雄被選為籌備人。對永雄來說，這雖然不是第一次擔任籌備人，不過這回要歡迎的是美國女性，他有些沒頭緒，於是和迪恩套交情，要求他幫忙。

永　雄：我剛接到新的任務。

迪　恩：喔？什麼任務？

永　雄：嗯，你應該知道有一位新同事要從芝加哥營業處調過來跟我們一起工作。

迪　恩：當然啦，我早就聽說了，她叫做喬伊·古柏，不過我完全不認識她。

永　雄：每次有新人加入我們的工作團隊，我們都會舉辦迎新會，而我被選派擔任這次的籌備人，也就是說，我得挑個地方，安排所有的瑣事。

迪　恩：祝你一切順利！

永　雄：謝啦，不過我在想……

迪　恩：想什麼？

永　雄：就是啊，就算你不認識古柏小姐，你一定還是比我更了解她會喜歡什麼吧。

迪　恩：我不是很確定吧！

永　雄：你教過我一句話，「做人要好心」，所以啦，你就行行好，幫我辦好這個迎新會吧。

迪　恩：不會吧！我？我這個小老頭兒？

永　雄：你身高六呎，一點都不矮小，而且你四十歲都不到，所以也不老。

迪　恩：好吧，算你贏了。我們該怎麼做？

永　雄：日期已經定好了，就是下禮拜二起算，再過兩個禮拜。所以我們要做的就是挑一個地方，然後決定菜單。

Dean: Don't we also have to decide on who'll be coming?

Nagao: Everyone in our section will be invited and I guess they'll all come.

Dean: How many will that make it?

Nagao: Oh, some ten people. Plus the President and some other top people—I guess we'll end up with some fifteen.

Dean: **As they say,** you can't go wrong with Chinese food.

Nagao: Think Ms. Cooper will like that best?

Dean: I'm sure she'll like it. Of course, some nice Japanese restaurant is another option.

Nagao: How about steak?

Dean: My guess is that she's had plenty of steak in Chicago and would probably welcome something different.

Nagao: There's a good Japanese place just a two-minute walk from here.

Dean: Well, **that's that**.

Nagao: Not quite. We'll have to go there, check it out and decide on the menu.

Dean: Well, I've come so far I'm ready to go all the way.

Nagao: I'm glad you're being a good guy.

Dean: By the way, who's paying for the party?

Nagao: Basically, the company is. But we'll probably have to pay some $1,000 each.

Dean: Good grief! I have to cough up one-thou?

Nagao: But you can help pick the menu.

Dean: Some compensation!

Nagao: O.K. You can collect the money at the door when the people come in. Won't that make you feel good?

Dean: Collecting money? Well, that'll make my day.* Say, does Joy know about the party?

迪　恩：不是還要決定參加人員的名單嗎？

永　雄：我們部門裡面每一個人都會受到邀請，我想他們應該會全員到齊。

迪　恩：那會有多少人？

永　雄：喔，大約十個人左右，再加上總裁還有一些高階幹部，我想總共差不多是十五個人。《some = about／top people = executives 管理者，主管》

迪　恩：一般來說，吃中國菜絕對錯不了。《go wrong with 出差錯》

永　雄：你覺得古柏小姐會最想吃中國菜嗎？

迪　恩：我敢說她一定會喜歡，當然啦，好吃的日本料理店也是另一種選擇。

永　雄：那牛排呢？

迪　恩：我猜她在芝加哥已經吃了很多牛排了，可能會想吃一些不一樣的。

永　雄：有一家不錯的日本料理店，離這裡走路只要兩分鐘。

迪　恩：那就決定那一家了。

永　雄：還沒啦，我們還得去一趟，確定一下，然後決定菜單。

迪　恩：好吧，都已經幫到這裡了，就幫你到底吧。

永　雄：我太高興了，你真是大好人啊！

迪　恩：對了，迎新會是誰出錢啊？

永　雄：基本上，公司會出錢。可是我們每個人可能還要交出一千元。

迪　恩：不會吧！我還得吐出一千塊喔？《cough up 不情願地拿出（錢）／one-thou = one thousand》

永　雄：不過你可以幫忙決定菜單啊。

迪　恩：好大的補償！〔反諷〕

永　雄：好吧，當大家進餐廳的時候，你還可以在門口幫我收錢，這樣有沒有感覺好一點？

迪　恩：收錢是吧？那太好了。對了，喬伊知道迎新會的事嗎？《Say = Listen, By the way》

Nagao: Of course not.

Dean: Why "of course not?"

Nagao: You don't tell people aɔout a welcoming party.

Dean: Why?

Nagao: I guess because they know.

Dean: You don't tell them but they know?

Nagao: You don't officially tell them but of course they find out or are told indirectly.

Dean: Well, that's great for Japanese but you can bet your bottom dollar that if nobody tells Joy about the party, she is not going to know.

Nagao: Maybe you're right. O.K., you tell her after she arrives.

Dean: Me? Good grief, little ole me?

Nagao: Sure, after all, you're a good guy, aren't you?

關鍵句

I've heard about it.	（這件事）我聽說了。
Good luck to you!	祝你好運！／一切順利！
I don't know about that.	我不知道。／（這件事）我不清楚。
Be a good guy.	行行好嘛。〈對象為男性〉
Good grief!	不會吧！／唉呀！
As they say,	一般認為～／一般來說～
That's that [it].	就這個了。／就這麼決定了。

永　雄：當然不知道啊。

迪　恩：為什麼會「當然不知道」?

永　雄：你不會跟一個當事人說我們要替他(她)辦迎新會吧?

迪　恩：為什麼?

永　雄：我想當事人都會知道啊。

迪　恩：你不告訴他們,他們怎麼會知道?

永　雄：就算沒有正式通知他們,他們也一定會知道,或是有人
　　　　會間接告訴他們。

迪　恩：嗯,這對日本人來說當然是沒問題,但是你要不要拿你
　　　　的老本賭賭看,如果沒有人跟她說的話,她是絕對不會
　　　　知道的。

永　雄：也許你說得沒錯,好吧,她來了以後你跟她說。

迪　恩：我? 不會吧! 又是我這個小老頭兒啊?

永　雄：當然是你囉,畢竟你是一個大好人嘛,不是嗎?

○ TIPS FOR EFFECTIVE COMMUNICATION ○

▶ that'll make my day (美國俚語)「那太好了」　直譯是「那
會讓我有愉快的一天」(此處為反諷)。make one's day是「使人
高興、快樂」的片語,出自克林·伊斯威特在電影「Dirty Harry
4」(1983年) 中,對著拿槍指著自己的敵人說: "Go ahead, make
my day!",從此成為名言。

14 淺談教會
WHAT TO DO AT CHURCH

Miho: Gee, I wonder what I should do this Sunday. I'm up-to-date with all my assignments; there's no good movie around; and my monthly allowance is almost all used up, and **I've nothing special to do**.

Grace: Why not just sleep late?

Miho: I can't sleep the whole day. What are you going to be doing?

Grace: Usually I go to church on Sundays.

Miho: I guess many Americans do. I've never gone to church.

Grace: Well, how about coming to church with me this Sunday?

Miho: I really wouldn't know what to do there. Besides, I'm not a Christian.

Grace: **That doesn't matter.** Just come and I'll tell you what to do. You just do what I do.

Miho: But what is it that you do in a church, pray?

Grace: Well, it depends on the church. In my church—it's a Methodist church—there are some prayers, some Bible reading; and we sing some hymns; there's an offering and our pastor preaches a sermon.

Miho: Anything else?

Grace: We have a good choir and you'll enjoy their singing. And some Sundays there's Holy Communion. That's when you take a small piece of bread and a little bit of wine as the symbols for the sacrifice of Jesus Christ.

> 美穗（20歲）高中畢業後便來到洛杉磯的大學留學，目前二年級，已經完全適應美國的生活，大學的課業雖然重，不過她倒是頗樂在其中。
>
> 這天上完課，美穗和好友葛瑞絲坐在學校的咖啡廳裡聊天，週末沒有安排計畫的美穗問起葛瑞絲週末有什麼打算，葛瑞絲說：「星期日要去教會，妳要不要一起來？」，從來沒去過教會的美穗有些遲疑……

美　穗：啊，我在想這個禮拜天要做什麼？該寫的功課都寫完了，也沒有什麼好看的電影，這個月的零用錢也差不多花完了，沒有什麼特別的事情好做。《allowance 零用錢》

葛瑞絲：為什麼不睡晚一點？

美　穗：總不能叫我睡一整天吧！那妳打算要做什麼？

葛瑞絲：通常我禮拜天會去教會。《on Sundays 每個禮拜天》

美　穗：我想很多美國人都是這樣，我從來沒有去過教會。

葛瑞絲：那這個禮拜天要不要跟我一起去？

美　穗：我真的不知道去那邊要做什麼，而且我也不是基督徒。

葛瑞絲：沒有關係的，妳儘管來就是了，我會跟妳說要怎麼做。我做什麼妳就跟著做什麼。

美　穗：可是妳去那邊都在做什麼，禱告嗎？

葛瑞絲：這個嘛，得看教會而定。我去的教會是衛理公會，會有一些禱告、讀經，還會唱一些聖歌、投奉獻，牧師也會講道。

美　穗：還有其他的嗎？

葛瑞絲：我們有一個很棒的唱詩班，妳一定會喜歡他們的歌聲。有時候禮拜天還有聖餐禮，就是吃一小塊麵包和喝一點葡萄酒，作做為耶穌蒙難的象徵。

14

Miho: I don't understand.

Grace: Not to worry. Just think of it as a ritual, a ceremony. How many people can really understand every detail about any ceremony?

Miho: Won't people be looking at me?

Grace: I don't think so. There are new faces almost every Sunday at my church and nobody would think of making a fuss. I'll be with you so you'll be comfortable.

Miho: Do all people go to church every Sunday?

Grace: I suppose you should; but I don't go every Sunday and my brother only goes a few times a year. You'd be surprised how many people only come for Christmas and Easter.

Miho: But I guess everyone's a Christian though.

Grace: It's not so simple. For example, I'm a Methodist. Methodists belong to one of the two big Christian groups,* the Protestants. Catholics are the other main group. Sometimes the two groups get along fine, but not always. Then, you know, there are Jews. There are millions of Jewish people, and they're certainly not Christians.

Miho: I see. So most people are Christians or Jews?

Grace: I guess so. In America, anyway. But **come to think of it**, there are many other religions here, like the Muslims.

Miho: In America?

Grace: Next time we go to lunch, I'll show you a small mosque.

Miho: Have you ever gone?

Grace: No, never have. **Come to think about it**, you probably know more about Christians than I know about Muslims.

Miho: I don't know much. I've never really studied anything about any religion. **Frankly, I can live without it.***

美　穗： 我聽不懂耶。

葛瑞絲： 別擔心，只要把它想成是一種典禮、一種儀式就可以了，有哪一個人能對所有儀式的每一個細節都瞭如指掌的？

美　穗： 別人不會注意我嗎？

葛瑞絲： 我想不至於吧，我們的教會幾乎每個禮拜天都有新面孔出現，沒有人會大驚小怪，而且有我跟妳在一起，妳可以放心。

美　穗： 大家每個禮拜都會上教堂嗎？

葛瑞絲： 我想應該是要的，不過我也沒有每個禮拜都去，像我弟弟一年只有去幾次而已。有很多人只有聖誕節和復活節才會去，很驚訝吧。

美　穗： 不過我想每個人都是基督教徒吧！

葛瑞絲： 沒有那麼單純。比方說，我就是衛理公會的會友，基督教有兩大教派，衛理公會是屬於其中的新教，另一個主要的教派就是天主教，有時候這兩大教派相安無事，但也不是永遠都這樣。還有，妳應該知道猶太教教徒吧，（在美國）有好幾百萬的猶太人，可是他們絕對不算基督徒。

美　穗： 我懂了，所以大部分的人都是基督徒或是猶太教教徒囉？

葛瑞絲： 我想是吧，至少在美國是這樣。不過仔細想一想，這裡倒是還有很多其他的宗教，像是回教徒。

美　穗： 妳是說在美國嗎？

葛瑞絲： 下次一起去吃午餐的時候，我再指給妳看，有一間小小的回教清真寺。

美　穗： 妳去過嗎？

葛瑞絲： 從來沒有。這樣想來，妳對基督教的了解，可能還超過我對回教的了解呢。

美　穗： 我知道的不多，我一向對任何宗教都沒有研究。坦白說，沒有宗教我也可以過得好好的。

Grace: **Different strokes for different folks.*** Anyway, I do hope you'll come with me this Sunday because this Sunday there's also going to be a church lunch.

Miho: I think I would like to go; it sounds like I would enjoy it.

Grace: It'll certainly be a worthwhile experience.

Miho: By the way, how should I dress? Are blue jeans O.K.?

Grace: I'd say **it's a no-no**. My church is a bit conservative about dressing. There's no fixed dress code but jeans and sandals aren't quite right.

Miho: I don't have formal clothes...

Grace: Doesn't need to be very formal. Anything neat will do.

Miho: I've got it. I'll wear my kimono.

Grace: Great! Everybody will love it. This Sunday, all eyes will be on Miho.

Miho: I'm happy.

Grace: Wait a minute, wait a minute. Didn't you say you didn't want people looking at you?

Miho: Well, nobody will be looking at me. They'll be looking at the kimono.

葛瑞絲： 見仁見智啦。 不管怎樣， 我真的希望這個禮拜天妳能跟
我一起去， 因為這個禮拜天我們教會將舉辦一個午餐聚
會。

美　穗： 我想我會去看一看，聽起來我應該會蠻喜歡的。

葛瑞絲： 一定會是個難得的經驗。

美　穗： 對了，我該怎麼穿？牛仔褲可以嗎？

葛瑞絲： 不可以的， 我們的教會對服裝有點保守，是沒有服裝上
的硬性規定，不過牛仔褲和涼鞋並不太適合。

美　穗： 我沒有正式的服裝……

葛瑞絲： 也不需要太正式啦，只要是乾淨整齊就可以了。

美　穗： 我想到了，我可以穿和服去。

葛瑞絲： 太好了！大家一定會很喜歡。這個禮拜天，所有人的目
光都會落在我們美穗身上。

美　穗： 真棒。

葛瑞絲： 等等！妳剛才不是說妳不希望別人一直看妳嗎？

美　穗： 嗯，沒有人會看我啊，他們看的是我的和服。

看著對方的眼睛

　　和人說話時，眼睛一定要看著對方，尤其是對於初次見面的人、長官、長輩，甚至是異性，說話時把視線瞥到一邊是很不禮貌的行為。英語圈習慣說話的時候看著對方，不敢直視談話者的人，不僅會被認為不禮貌，有時還會給人不值得信賴的印象。看著對方的眼睛(make eye contact)可以傳達出「我有在聽你說」、「對你的話題感興趣」，所以說膽子小的人一定要訓練自己，一開始可能有點不好意思，但是很快就會習慣的。（直盯著對方瞧也不行，可別過頭了。）

關鍵句

I've nothing special to do.	我沒有什麼特別的事情好做。
That [It] doesn't matter.	沒關係。
Come to think of [about] it,	仔細想一想～
Frankly (speaking),	坦白說～
I can live without it.	沒有～我也能過得很好。
Different strokes for different folks.	見仁見智。／人各有志。
It's a no-no.	（絕對）不可以。

◦ TIPS FOR EFFECTIVE COMMUNICATION ◦

▶ the two big Christian groups 「基督教兩大教派」 基督教在北美大致分成兩派，一是Catholic [`kæθəlɪk] Church （天主教），一是Protestant [`prɑtɪstənt] Church（新教）。原先最早只有天主教，後來德國的馬丁·路德因為不滿天主教的許多作法，另行在1517年創設了新教。新教後來又分成許多denomination

（教派），幾個主要的有：Baptist Church（浸信會），Presbyterian Church（長老教會），United Church（聯合兄弟會），Lutheran Church（路德教會），Episcopal Church（聖公會）等。

▶ I can live without it. 「沒有～我也可以過得好好的」 意思是「不感興趣、不需要、不喜歡」的玩笑式說法，有時也作委婉回答，例如："Do you like cheese?" "Well, I can live without it."（「你喜歡起司嗎?」「我沒有它也行」）。

▶ Different strokes for different folks. strokes是「方法、手段」，folks是「人們」，兩個字押韻，意思是「每個人的作法（想法）不同」。例如：A: "To keep in shape, I run everyday."（我每天跑步以保持身材） B: "I think swimming is much better."（我覺得游泳比較好） A: "Well, different strokes for different folks."（每個人的作法不同）。

15 成田機場的老問題
THE PERENNIAL PROBLEM OF NARITA

Victor: Well, **I'm off next week**.

Eric: You're off?

Victor: Yep. I'm off to home, sweet home.

Eric: How come?

Victor: My brother is getting married so I've got permission to attend the wedding.

Eric: **Lucky you.**

Victor: That's how I feel.

Eric: Are they covering your ticket?

Victor: No. **They wouldn't go that far.**

Eric: And you're off via Narita.

Victor: Sure. There's no other way to go, is there?

Eric: No. Not unless you go to Osaka and then you've got the bullet train fare.

Victor: Narita's **not so bad**.

Eric: Not so bad? Just getting there costs a pretty penny.

Victor: True, it's not cheap.

Eric: And then the time, the trouble, the aggravation.

Victor: True, it does take time.

Eric: About half a day.

> 威克特（36歲）和艾瑞克（38歲）是東京某大證券公司的同事，兩人都是美國人，來日本都已經超過五年。某天早上，兩人在公司走廊上碰到，原本只打算聊個幾句，沒想到一聊就聊了好久。
>
> 威克特先是提到在美國的弟弟要結婚了，打算請一個星期的有薪休假回去參加他的婚禮。艾瑞克問他打算從哪個機場離境，又說去成田機場的交通既耗時間又浪費金錢，兩人繞著這個話題談了好久。最後，威克特似乎找到了前往成田機場的最佳方法。

威克特： 嗯，我下禮拜放假。

艾瑞克： 放假？

威克特： 是啊，我要回家，回我可愛的故鄉。《Yep [jɛp] = Yes》

艾瑞克： 為什麼？《How come? = Why?》

威克特： 我弟弟要結婚了，所以我獲准放假，好參加他的婚禮。

艾瑞克： 真好運。

威克特： 我也這麼覺得。

艾瑞克： 他們有幫你出機票錢嗎？《cover 支出》

威克特： 沒有，公司才不會管這麼多。

艾瑞克： 那你是要在成田機場搭機囉。

威克特： 當然啦，沒有其他方法了不是嗎？

艾瑞克： 是啊，除非你從大阪出去，不過那樣你還得花子彈列車的車費。

威克特： 成田機場也沒有那麼糟啦。

艾瑞克： 沒有那麼糟？光是去那邊就要花很多錢了。《a pretty penny 一大筆錢》

威克特： 沒錯，是不便宜。

艾瑞克： 而且既花時間又麻煩，心情也變得不好。

威克特： 沒錯，真的很浪費時間。

艾瑞克： 差不多要半天的時間。

Victor: Anyway, it's not so bad. Now there are two trains that go direct to the airport building.

Eric: But have you tried to lug your luggage to those trains?

Victor: **You got a point.**

Eric: Of course, if you live near Ueno, you can catch the Skyliner and that's not so expensive. But if you don't...

Victor: **On top of all that**, you've got to reserve early to be sure of getting a seat.

Eric: And if you try to find the Narita Express platform at Tokyo Station, well, it's an experience.*

Victor: An experience?

Eric: An experience to be avoided at all costs. Following the signs is like entering a mysterious maze. It's horrendous!

Victor: Maybe I should go from Yokohama.

Eric: Yokohama is easier. But more expensive. And there are fewer trains.

Victor: Well, what should I do?

Eric: Try TCAT, you know, the Tokyo City Air Terminal in Hakozaki. You can check your baggage and get everything over with right there.

Victor: Great! **That's for me.**

Eric: But...

Victor: But? What's the but?

Eric: But many cheap tickets don't let you check in at TCAT.

Victor: Who said I'm getting a cheap ticket?

Eric: If you're going to have to pay, I'd say you're going hunting for an el cheapo ticket.

威克特： 不管怎樣，還不算太差啦，現在有兩班電車直達機場大廳。

艾瑞克： 可是你有過奮力拖著行李進電車的經驗嗎？

威克特： 被你說到重點了。

艾瑞克： 當然啦，假如你住在上野附近，就可以搭Skyliner，那還不會太貴，可是如果你不是的話……

威克特： 除了這些之外，還得早早訂票，才會有位子。

艾瑞克： 而且如果到了東京車站，要找到成田機場的快車月臺，嗯，那真是個難忘的經驗。

威克特： 難忘的經驗？

艾瑞克： 那是個說什麼也要避免的經驗。你跟著指標一路走，就好像走進一座神祕的迷宮，真是太恐怖了。

《horrendous = awful 糟透了的》

威克特： 也許我應該從橫濱回去。

艾瑞克： 從橫濱就比較容易了，不過比較貴就是了，而且火車的班次也比較少。

威克特： 嗯，那我該怎麼辦？

艾瑞克： 你可以試試看TCAT（唸法為T-CAT）啊，就是位在箱崎的Tokyo City Air Terminal（東京都航空站），那裡就可以託運行李，而且可以把所有的事情一次辦好。《check 寄存[託運]行李》

威克特： 太好了！這個適合我。

艾瑞克： 可是……

威克特： 可是？還有什麼可是？

艾瑞克： 可是很多便宜的機票是不讓你在TCAT登機的。

威克特： 誰說我要買便宜機票了？

艾瑞克： 如果機票錢要你自己出的話，我敢說你一定會找便宜的機票來買。《el cheapo 廉價的》

15

Victor: If it gets down to brass tacks...?*

Eric: And the nitty-gritty...?*

Victor: You're right. I like cheap.*

Eric: So what do you do?

Victor: Right. What do I do?

Eric: Suffer.

Victor: No alternative?

Eric: None.

Victor: You know what I love about talking with you?

Eric: I can guess.

Victor: **You're a help.** You make people feel better.

Eric: **You misjudge me.** Everyone misjudges me.

Victor: Is that so?

Eric: You're damned tootin', it's so.* Tell you what I'm going to do.

Victor: **Spare me.**

Eric: I am going to drive you right to the airport. Now, what have you got to say to that?

Victor: It's going to rain.*

Eric: It's going to rain? It's going to rain? Come on, you've been in Japan much too long.

Victor: But you've been here longer that I have.

Eric: Which is lucky for you. If I hadn't been in Japan too long, you wouldn't be getting a ride to Narita.

Victor: Well, you're a good guy after all.

威克特： 如果回到正題……

艾瑞克： 回到現實面……

威克特： 你說得沒錯，我是喜歡買便宜的。

艾瑞克： 那你怎麼辦？

威克特： 對喔，我該怎麼辦？

艾瑞克： 就忍一下囉！

威克特： 沒有其他的選擇了嗎？

艾瑞克： 沒有。

威克特： 你知道我喜歡跟你說話的原因嗎？

艾瑞克： 我可以猜得到。

威克特： 你真是一個好幫手〔反諷〕，你讓別人覺得事情都沒有那麼糟。

艾瑞克： 你誤解我了，大家都誤解我了。

威克特： 是這樣嗎？

艾瑞克： 一點也沒錯，就是這樣。告訴你我打算怎麼做好了。

威克特： 得了吧。

艾瑞克： 我打算直接載你去機場，那你現在還有什麼話說？

威克特： 喲，是天要下雨了不成。(It's going to rain.→這是從日文直譯而來的俏皮話，英語中沒有這種說法)

艾瑞克： 天要下雨？什麼是天要下雨？喔，真服了你，你來日本真的太久了。

威克特： 可是你比我還久。

艾瑞克： 所以算你走運，要是我沒在日本待那麼久，就不可能載你到成田機場了。《get a ride 搭便車》

威克特： 嗯，原來你也是一個好人。

15

當個好聽眾

「自然的會話節奏(a natural conversational flow)」是會話時的一項重要因素，除了想自己要講的話，還要專心聽對方說話，並且適時作反應，這樣對話才會投機。像是Wow! / Oh, really? / Not really. / That's it. / Sure. / Is that so? / I know. / Great!等短句，雖然沒什麼意思，卻能炒熱氣氛，十分好用。除此之外，一些意味深遠的應和句子，你也可以在本書中找到。

關鍵句

I'm off next week.	我下禮拜休假。
Lucky you.	你真好運。／算你走運。
They wouldn't go that far.	他們不會做那麼多。
Not so bad.	也沒有那麼糟啦!／也沒有那麼差。
You got a point.	你說到重點了。
On top of all that,	除了這些之外～
That's for me.	這個適合我。
You're a help.	你真是個好幫手。
You misjudge me.	你誤解我了。
Spare me.	你省省吧!／得了吧!

○ *TIPS FOR EFFECTIVE COMMUNICATION* ○

▶ it's an experience 「真是個難忘的經驗」 也就是an experience that you won't be able to forget，通常用在不好的方面。

▶ If it gets down to brass tacks... (口語)「如果回到正題」這裡的「正題」指的是上文提到的「如果錢要自己出的話」，後文接的可能是I'll buy the cheapest one.。 get down to brass tacks是個片語，意思是「進入正題，觸及問題的核心」，是由brass tacks (黃銅圖釘)的功用 (固定東西)為出發點演變而來。

▶ the nitty-gritty... (口語)「回到現實面」 get [come] down to the nitty-gritty是個片語，用法和上面的brass tacks相同。 the nitty-gritty指的是「核心、正題、嚴峻的現實、具體的一面」等等，可作名詞或形容詞，經常出現在會話中。

▶ I like cheap. 「我是喜歡便宜」 如果以文法來說，這句話是有問題的，不過會話中經常使用，不妨把它想成是I like things that are cheap.的省略。

▶ You're damned tootin', it's so. (俚語)「一點也沒錯」You're damned tootin'.是句慣用語，意思是「就是這樣，完全正確」，後頭的it's so指的是"Everyone misjudges me."。

▶ It's going to rain. 這是從日文直譯而來的一句英語，相當於中文的「太陽從西邊出來」、「天要下紅雨了」。會話中的兩位主角是在日本居住很久的外國人，算是日語通，所以彼此都懂得這句笑話。當然，英語裡是沒有這種說法的。幽默以及玩笑話是英語文化的一部分，這也是我們在學習英語時，必須有的基本認識。

16

露營與杓子
HISHAKU AND CAMPING

Kurt: There's a three-day weekend rolling in. What are you going to do?

Gary: Well, I'd really like to go out, away from it all. But with the wife and two kids, it'll cost a small fortune. I'm stumped.

Kurt: We're going camping.

Gary: Camping? You know, somehow I don't think of you as Daniel Boone.*

Kurt: **No way.** When we go, we go in style. Good cheese, wine...the whole works.

Gary: I don't know. I once passed what they call here an "auto-camp" place and had a look. And from what I saw, I'd just as soon be at Shinjuku Station.*

Kurt: I can imagine what you saw.

Gary: Everybody pitched their tent right next to their car. It's as if being separated from their car would be as traumatic as cutting an umbilical cord. Some people even attached part of their tent fly to the car.

Kurt: I've seen the same thing.

Gary: And the tent sites were so close together I could swear some people were sharing pegs!

科特（36歲）和蓋瑞（40歲）在東京同一所大學教美國文學，兩人正巧都是佛蒙特州的人，也都喜歡戶外生活，感情想當然地特別好。

有一天，兩人趁著課餘空檔聊天，話題是即將到來的三天連假。科特說他打算去露營，蓋瑞聽到後的反應是「露營是不錯啦，可是……」，看來他對市郊那些露營場地的擁擠情形不是很滿意，意願似乎不高。

科　特：這個週末三天的假期馬上就要到了，你打算要做什麼？

蓋　瑞：嗯，我真的很想出去走一走，遠離俗世。可是加上我太太和兩個小孩，就要花上一筆錢，真不知道該怎麼辦？《away from it all 擺脫日常俗事》

科　特：我們要去露營。

蓋　瑞：露營？你知道嗎？不知道為什麼我就是沒辦法把你想像成（拓荒者）丹尼爾‧布恩。

科　特：當然不是啊。我們去的話，是悠閒的去，上好的起司，美酒……所有的一切。

蓋　瑞：不知道該怎麼說，有一次我經過日本人所謂的「汽車露營」營地，我看了一下，而就我所看到的，那乾脆去新宿車站好了。《auto-camp 是日本人自創的英語，正確的說法應該是car camping》

科　特：我可以想像你看到的畫面。

蓋　瑞：那裡的每一個人就地在汽車旁邊搭帳篷，好像他們如果跟車子分開的話，就會像割斷臍帶一樣受傷似的，有些人甚至就把帳篷上面那層（下大雨時用的）罩布繫在車上。

科　特：我也看過同樣的畫面。

蓋　瑞：而且營地擠得很，我敢發誓，帳篷的椿一定也是很多人一起共用！

Kurt: Many, maybe most camp grounds in Japan are like that. But not all.

Gary: **That's good news.**

Kurt: I grant you it took time. We looked and looked and finally we did find a few nice spots, like one in Tanzawa where tent sites aren't even marked. You simply pick a nice spot and as often as not, no one's nearby.

Gary: **I'm all ears.**

Kurt: And there's a place near Nikko where you have to drag all your stuff from the car and walk about ten minutes. That's more than enough to discourage most of your car campers.* We see more deer than people there.

Gary: I didn't think they had places like that here.

Kurt: But don't expect anything fancy. Just a water faucet and an outhouse, your basic john. If it's fancy, it's crowded, and expensive.

Gary: **I'm on your wave length.** Why travel from Tokyo to go camping unless you can feel free and easy with nature all around?

Kurt: You got a tent I guess.

Gary: It's not terribly big though. I developed a system: a small, waterproof tent with a full fly, and an enormous tarp. That way we can cook and enjoy ourselves even if it rains.

Kurt: We have a big tent and a small tarp.

Gary: The only trouble with the big tarp is setting it up so it doesn't sag. If it sags, the rain accumulates and the tarp collapses, a real disaster which, I'm sorry to say, I've experienced.

Kurt: I indulge myself with real goodies. But I've never found a

科　特：是很多人共用沒錯，　日本大部分的露營場地可能都像這樣，不過並不是全部都是這樣。

蓋　瑞：這可真是好消息。

科　特：我承認是要花點時間，　不過我們找了又找，　最後真的找到了一些不錯的地點，像Tanzawa（日本地名：丹澤）有一個地方，　那裡的營地甚至都還沒有標示出來。只要你找到一個不錯的地點，　通常都不會有其他人。《mark 標示》

蓋　瑞：我洗耳恭聽。

科　特：還有一個地方，　在日光附近，　你得辛苦搬著車上所有的東西走差不多十分鐘才會到，　這樣就足以讓很多汽車露營的人打退堂鼓了。　在那裡看到的鹿比看到的人還要多。《drag 拖曳》

蓋　瑞：沒想到（日本）竟然有這種地方。

科　特：不過也不要想得太美好，　那兒就只有一個水龍頭，和一個戶外廁所，　最簡陋的那種。如果要享受的話，一定是人擠人，而且所費不貲。《basic john 設備原始的廁所》

蓋　瑞：君子所見略同。　要是不能放鬆心情徜徉在大自然的話，那幹嘛離開東京去露營？

科　特：我猜你應該有帳篷。

蓋　瑞：有是有，不過不是很大。我研究出一套方法，一頂不大的防水帳篷加上全罩式的覆布，　再加上一片超大的防水布，這樣一來，就算下雨，我們還是可以（在防水布下）炊煮食物，玩得很盡興。《tarp 防水帆布》

科　特：我們家有一個大帳篷和一小塊的防水布。

蓋　瑞：大片防水布最大的麻煩，　就是要固定好才不會塌下來，萬一塌下來的話，　上面積的雨水就會連同防水布一起塌下來，那真是天大的災難，不瞞你說，我就有過這樣的經驗。《sag 下垂、凹陷》

科　特：我特別喜歡享受美食，　可是我從來沒有找到一張看起來

decent looking table that was big enough to eat from in comfort. So I ended up making one myself.

Gary: So you're a handyman?

Kurt: Well, I admit **I'm into** tables. I even made a small one for the tent. I took those fold-down little legs they use for tatami tables and attached them to a nice piece of wood that I stained. Those legs are just right for a tent: after all, they're made not to mar the tatami so naturally they don't scratch the tent floor.

Gary: Why a table inside a tent?

Kurt: Ever put a glass of whiskey on a tent floor? Or anything else? **Sooner or later**, it'll spill and you've got a mess. It's also ideal for a fluorescent lantern or candle.

Gary: You should patent it. Never heard of a table for a tent.

Kurt: Makes sense. There's a lot of things nobody has come up with yet. Like a good container for water.

Gary: Come on. There's hundreds of those around.

Kurt: Maybe there are. But all of them are either too small—so you have to go and fill them up too often. Or too big—and water is quite heavy. And then how do you get the water out? Just where do you put that big heavy water container so you can easily get water out?

Gary: Now don't laugh but my wife came up with a great idea. You know those small dippers or scoops with long handles that you find at every shrine? Well, we take one of those along. It's perfect for scooping boiling water out of a big pot for coffee or soup or just to wash the plates.

Kurt: Ingenious. Now there's an item that you just are not going to find even in the most complete camping catalog from any company in the States.

很氣派的桌子，大到可以舒舒服服地用餐，所以最後我就自己做了一張。

蓋　瑞：看不出來你還是一個會手工藝的人。《handyman 手巧、會自己動手修修補補、做東西的男人》

科　特：嗯，我承認我對桌子很感興趣，我還做了一張帳篷裡面專用的小桌子。我拿來了榻榻米矮桌用的那種摺疊式桌腳，然後固定到一塊上好的木頭上，我還自己上色，那些桌腳的高度正好適合放在帳篷裡面，畢竟，那些桌腳的設計，就是不要刮壞榻榻米，所以自然也就不會刮傷帳篷的底部。《mar 損傷 / scratch 刮傷》

蓋　瑞：為什麼帳篷裡面要放桌子？

科　特：你有沒有放一杯威士忌在帳篷的地板上過？或是其他的東西呢？遲早它都會灑出來，弄得一團糟。而且，在桌上放一個螢光燈（籠）或是蠟燭也很理想。

蓋　瑞：你應該申請專利，從來就沒有聽說有帳篷專用的桌子。

科　特：有道理。還有很多東西都還沒有人想出來，比方說裝水的容器。

蓋　瑞：拜託，多得是咧。《There's = There're》

科　特：也許是有人發明啦，不過不是太大就是太小，太小的就要常常去裝水，太大的話，裝了水又很重，還有把水取出來也是個問題，真不知道這麼笨重的裝水容器該放在哪裡，取水才會方便。

蓋　瑞：嗯，不要笑喔，我太太想了一個不錯的方法。你知道那些長柄的舀水小杓子吧，就是在每一個神社都看得到的那一種。我們就帶上一支，可以把煮沸的水從大壺裡舀出來，可以泡茶、泡咖啡，或是洗盤子也可以，非常好用。《dipper 長柄杓 / scoop〔名詞〕杓子；〔動詞〕舀取》

科　特：真是天才！就算是美國任何一家公司所提供的最完整的露營用品型錄，也找不到這種東西。

16

Gary: Who said there aren't advantages to living in Japan?

關鍵句

No way.	完全錯誤。／不對吧。
That's good news.	這真是好消息。
I'm all ears.	我洗耳恭聽。
I'm on your wave length.	我同意你的看法。／我的意見和你相同。
I'm into ～.	我對～很感興趣。
Sooner or later,	遲早～

蓋　瑞：誰說住在日本沒有什麼好處?

○ TIPS FOR EFFECTIVE COMMUNICATION ○

▶ Daniel Boone （1734–1820)美國，尤其是肯塔基州的拓荒者， 西部墾荒史上的重要道路Wilderness Road， 以及Boonesboro的開闢者，在美國墾荒史中佔有一定地位。他的名字後來成為在開墾地大有作為者的代名詞,註冊商標是頭上經常戴著一頂海狸帽（上面垂著一條長尾巴）。

▶ I'd just as soon be at Shinjuku Station.「（與其待在那樣的汽車營地）那乾脆去新宿車站好了」 Shinjuku Station後頭省略了as be at that "auto-camp" place。would [had] (just) as soon A (as B)是「與其從事B不如從事A」的片語。

▶ That's more than enough to discourage most of your car campers. 「這樣就足以讓很多汽車露營的人打退堂鼓了」That指的是前面提到的下了車還要走十分鐘的路程。

17 清談
THE VERY PINK OF A CONVERSATION

Mark: Tell me, what's your favorite season?

Philip: Well, I guess it's fall.

Mark: Me, I like the spring when everything starts to grow again.

Philip: I prefer fall; it's a quiet time; the weather is just right and the colors of the leaves on the trees are so, well, extraordinary.

Mark: The colors may be nice but you haven't seen any pink leaves, have you?

Philip: Pink?* No, **come to think of it,** no pink.

Mark: But in spring, the cherry blossoms and plum blossoms are the most exquisite, delicate pink you can imagine.

Philip: I'll admit that if you like pink, spring may be best.

Mark: You don't care for pink?

Philip: Well no; **let me tell you** that I'm no pinko.

Mark: Pinko? Who's talking about politics? Besides, since **you raised the subject,** don't you like to be in the pink?

Philip: Very funny. You *are* a card. Next you're going to tell me that you only wear pinked clothes.

Mark: No, I'm not going to say that but I'll bet you never put a pink in your lapel.

Philip: What is this? The punning hour? Or are you preparing a monograph on the Pinkertons?

馬克（26歲）和菲力浦（29歲）是東京某英文報社的記者。馬克來日本兩年，菲力浦則將近三年，兩人都喜歡說笑，尤其喜歡文字遊戲。

這天休息時間，兩人又開始不著邊際的「清談」，話題從季節聊到「粉紅」，然後是感恩節、火雞等等，越說越離譜了……

馬　克：告訴我，你最喜歡的季節是什麼？

菲力浦：嗯，我想是秋天吧。

馬　克：我的話，最喜歡春天，萬物開始生長的時候。

菲力浦：我比較喜歡秋天，很寧靜、氣候宜人，而且樹上葉子的顏色也是……怎麼說呢，那麼的特別。

馬　克：顏色可能不錯，不過你沒看過粉紅色的樹葉吧，有嗎？

菲力浦：粉紅色？沒有耶，仔細想一下，還真是沒看過。

馬　克：可是在春天，櫻花、梅花都是你想像中那種最高雅、最嬌嫩的粉紅色。

菲力浦：我承認如果你喜歡粉紅色的話，春天也許最適合。

馬　克：你不喜歡粉紅色？

菲力浦：嗯，不喜歡，而且跟你說，我不是左傾分子。《pinko〔輕蔑語〕左翼分子》

馬　克：左傾分子？誰跟你談政治了？而且，既然你提到這個話題，難道你不喜歡精神飽滿嗎？《in the pink 健康，精神飽滿》

菲力浦：真好笑──你真是個笑話高手。你接下來要跟我說你只穿鋸齒狀的衣服對吧。《pinked 用鋸齒狀的剪刀剪裁的》

馬　克：才不是，我才不是要說這個。我想說的是，我敢打賭，你一定從來沒在翻領上佩帶過粉紅色的花。《lapel 衣服的翻領》

菲力浦：我們這是在幹嘛？雙關語時間嗎？還是你準備了關於the Pinkertons的專題論文？《punning 說雙關語的 / Pinkerton美國第一家私人偵探社》

Mark: How corny.

Philip: Right, corn. Corn for which we can thank the Native American Indians. That's what Thanksgiving is all about.

Mark: What kind of a conversation is this? How did we get from the Pinkertons to Thanksgiving? But I'll tell you this: I wonder if native American Indians today are so terribly happy about Thanksgiving.

Philip: I'm happy about Thanksgiving. It's a holiday, a great excuse to eat some delicious turkey and cranberries. I only eat cans of "whole style" cranberry sauce; you can keep that smooth style. Even I, though, have given up on fresh whole cranberries. I tried them once. Though I cooked them with lots of sugar, they were still so sour that my tongue curled up.

Mark: Look, I know you like to go off on a tangent. But just what has all this to do with the seasons?

Philip: You're asking me? You started with the seasons, remember?

Mark: **As a matter of fact,** I don't remember.

Philip: Well, I do remember and there is a connection because the time to eat turkey and cranberries is now, in the fall, at Thanksgiving.

Mark: You know, I can't understand why if something is no good, if it's a used car or a bad movie, we say it's a turkey or a lemon. Just what do a turkey and a lemon have in common?

Philip: **I don't have the faintest idea.**

Mark: I mean, one's an animal and one's a fruit.

Philip: Right.

Mark: One's brownish and flies and the other's yellow and sits on a tree.

Philip: **You're sharp today.**

Mark: So come on, help me out.

馬　克：真是老套。《corny 陳腐的》

菲力浦：沒錯，不過老套讓我想到玉米，就是因為玉米，我們才能夠感謝美國印地安人，這就是感恩節的重點。

馬　克：這是哪門子的對話啊？我們怎麼從the Pinkertons跳到感恩節去啦？不過我想跟你說，我很懷疑現今美國印地安人是不是仍然歡度感恩節。

菲力浦：我倒是很喜歡過感恩節，那天是假日，還可以藉機吃一些美味的火雞和蔓越莓。我只吃有整顆果粒的罐裝蔓越莓果醬，那種糊糊的果醬就留給你好了。我雖然不吃新鮮的蔓越莓，不過我以前吃過一次，即便我加了很多糖一起煮，但還是很酸，害我舌頭都捲成一團。《you can keep～ ～就給你好了，我不要～ / curl up 捲曲》

馬　克：聽著，我知道你很喜歡扯東扯西的，可是這些跟四季到底有什麼關係？

菲力浦：你問我？是你開始講到季節的耶，你忘了嗎？

馬　克：實際上，我真的忘了。

菲力浦：好吧，我還記得。這之間是有關聯的，因為吃火雞和蔓越莓的時機就是現在，就是秋天，就是感恩節。

馬　克：你知道嗎？我不知道為什麼一個東西很爛，比如說是二手車或是很難看的電影，我們就說它是火雞或是檸檬，真不知道火雞和檸檬有什麼共通性？

菲力浦：我一點概念也沒有。

馬　克：我是說，一個是動物，一個是水果。《one's = one is》

菲力浦：沒錯。

馬　克：一個是棕色的，還會飛；另一個卻是黃色的，長在樹上。

菲力浦：你今天說話還真是犀利啊！〔反諷〕

馬　克：得了吧，快點幫我想一下。

Philip: Help you out? I just told you that I don't have the faintest idea what the two have in common. How can I help you out?

Mark: Well, you'd better come up with something, or this conversation is rapidly going to come to an end.

Philip: I'm prepared to accept that.

Mark: Well, then, **that's that**.

《《關鍵句》》

Come to think of it,	仔細想想～
Let me tell you.	跟你說喔。／告訴你好了。
You raised the subject.	是你開始這個話題的。
As a matter of fact,	實際上／事實上
I don't have the faintest idea.	我一點概念也沒有。
You're sharp (today).	你（今天）說話很犀利。
That's that. (= That's it.)	就這樣吧。／就這麼決定了。

菲力浦： 幫你想一下什麼？ 我剛才跟你說啦， 這兩者有什麼共通
　　　　 點， 我一點概念也沒有， 你要我怎麼幫你想？

馬　克： 嗯， 你最好想點什麼話題， 不然的話， 這次的對話很快
　　　　 就會結束了。

菲力浦： 我已做好準備了。

馬　克： 嗯， 那就這樣吧。

◦ TIPS FOR EFFECTIVE COMMUNICATION ◦

▶ Pink? 「粉紅色?」 pink除了顏色之外，還有許多意思。其
中最主要的有： 1)蠶麥、康乃馨等蠶麥科石竹屬的植物總稱。
2)(the pink)極致、絕頂。例如： in the pink (of health [condition])
「非常健康」（本文中的用法）。3)(pinko)左翼分子。另外，pink
作動詞時有「使～成鋸齒狀」的意思 （pinking scissors「有鋸
齒的剪刀」 就是由此而來）。 馬克與菲力浦就是以這些含義的
pink為題材， 互相捉弄對方。

18 淡季比較好玩?
IS OFF-SEASON MORE FUN?

Julia: Booked yet for the holidays?

Eve: No. I'm in no rush.

Julia: **If I were you,** I start looking around. The flights fill up pretty quickly when it comes to Christmas and New Year's.

Eve: I agree; if I were you, that's what I would do. But I'm not.

Julia: You're not what?

Eve: I'm not you.

Julia: **Suit yourself.** Only trying to be helpful.

Eve: I'm sorry. It's just that when most people say "if I were you" it isn't much help since you're not me and the only way to really be helpful is to put yourself in *my* shoes, not put me in yours. It's just a pet peeve of mine. **Forget it.**

Julia: What you say does make sense. But anyway, what are you doing for the holidays? I'm headed back home for a wonderful Christmas dinner with my folks in Richmond, Virginia.

Eve: I kind of envy you. Christmas in Japan is the pits. But what could be more fun than New Year's in Tokyo?

Julia: You mean you're staying here?

Eve: Certainly for New Year's.

茱麗亞(29歲)和伊芙(27歲)都是美國人,同在東京某貿易公司上班,兩人一前一後到日本大約有四年的時間,目前都是小姑獨處。

十一月中旬的某個午後,兩人喝著咖啡,談論年假打算怎麼過。茱麗亞說她要回美國和家人團聚,伊芙則有些龜毛,最討厭和別人一窩蜂的她,打算待在東京,享受難得的空城……

茱麗亞: 這次放假訂位了嗎?《Booked = Have you booked / book 預訂座位》

伊　芙: 還沒,我一點都不急。

茱麗亞: 如果我是妳, 早就張大眼睛開始注意了, 聖誕節和新年假期的航班很快就滿了。《New Year's = New Year's holidays》

伊　芙: 我同意,如果我是妳的話,我是會這樣做,不過我又不是。

茱麗亞: 妳又不是什麼?

伊　芙: 我又不是妳。

茱麗亞: 隨妳便,我只是想幫上一點忙。《Only = I'm only》

伊　芙: 很抱歉,只是很多人在講「如果我是妳」這種話的時候,其實是幫不上什麼忙的, 因為妳又不是我, 唯一幫得上忙的方法, 應該是站在我的立場, 而不是要我依照妳的看法去做。 我只是對這種事很厭煩, 妳不要放在心上。《a pet peeve 惱人的小事》

茱麗亞: 妳說得很有道理。 不過, 妳這個假期到底要做什麼? 我要回我在維吉尼亞州里奇蒙的老家, 和家人吃一頓豐盛的聖誕節大餐。《be headed back home 回故鄉》

伊　芙: 我有點羨慕妳。 聖誕節待在日本簡直糟透了, 可是如果是新年的話, 東京就好玩得不得了。

茱麗亞: 妳是說妳要待在這裡?

伊　芙: 新年的話是一定會的。

Julia: I thought New Year's is when every place is so crowded and expensive that you'd hate it.

Eve: You're basically right. But it's the week around New Year's when everybody *leaves* Tokyo. I discovered that there's no better time to enjoy Tokyo than during New Year's. It's about the only chance you get to drive freely through Tokyo without a single traffic jam. Whatever movies, restaurants, temples, or parks are open, you can go and really take it easy.

Julia: I almost forgot: you're the off-season girl. Whatever the place, if it's a seaside resort or a special restaurant, when it's off-season it's on for you.

Eve: I guess you're right. When it's off-season, it's always cheaper and certainly less crowded.

Julia: I'm sure it is. But isn't it also less fun?

Eve: Maybe. But not in my book. You know, another pet peeve of mine is that I just don't like the herd instinct. People moving in masses from one place to another and trying to push me along with them drive me up the wall.*

Julia: I don't think anyone's pushing you. And I still think off-season is less fun. Of course it's easy to get around Tokyo during New Year's because there's no one here. I mean it's dead so **what's the point**? I'm the first one to say "different strokes for different folks" but...

Eve: But you simply can't make sense of what I like to do?

Julia: That's it in a nutshell.

Eve: To tell you the truth, sometimes I can't make sense of what I do either.

Julia: Are you absolutely gung-ho on staying here over the holidays?

Eve: Frankly, I just don't have many other options this year.

茱麗亞： 我以為新年到處都是人擠人，消費又高，妳會不喜歡。

伊　芙： 基本上妳說對了。不過，過年的那個禮拜大家都離開東
　　　　 京，我發現要享受東京的生活，最好的時間就是過年那
　　　　 一段假期了，那可能是唯一可以在東京自由自在開車的
　　　　 機會，而且絕對不會塞車。電影、餐廳、寺廟、公園也
　　　　 都有開，可以徹底放鬆一下。

茱麗亞： 我差點忘了，妳是「淡季女孩」，不管什麼地方，海濱勝
　　　　 地也好，特別的餐廳也好，淡季一到才是你的旺季。
　　　　 《off-season 淡季的，時令不對的》

伊　芙： 被妳說中了，淡季的時候，價格都會比較便宜，人也比
　　　　 較少。

茱麗亞： 是這樣沒錯，可是樂趣不是也少一點嗎？

伊　芙： 也許吧，不過我可不這麼認為。另外一件讓我生氣的呢，
　　　　 就是我不喜歡人類群居的本能，大家一窩蜂從一個地方
　　　　 衝到另一個地方，還想強迫我隨波逐流，真是令人不爽。

茱麗亞： 我想沒有人在強迫妳。我還是覺得淡季的時候沒那麼好
　　　　 玩，當然過年的時候在東京到處逛是很悠閒沒錯，因為
　　　　 沒有人嘛。我是說這樣不就死氣沈沈的，有什麼好玩呢？
　　　　 雖然我絕對同意「人各有志」，不過……

伊　芙： 不過妳就是不能理解我這樣做道理何在？

茱麗亞： 簡單講就是這樣。

伊　芙： 老實跟妳說，有時候我自己也不知道這樣做有什麼道理。

茱麗亞： 妳是一心想要整個假期都待在這裡嗎？《gung-ho 狂熱的》

伊　芙： 坦白說，我今年實在沒什麼選擇。

Julia: Have you ever been to Richmond?

Eve: No.

Julia: Look. Why don't you come home with me? My parents would love to have you. There are a lot of fun things to do, even a first-class Vietnamese restaurant. Come on, join my crowd.

Eve: You're really sweet. Besides, going to Richmond in the winter is a bit off-season anyway. Let me ring my travel agent first thing tomorrow.

Julia: **Now you're talking.**

(((關鍵句)))

If I were you,	如果我是你的話～
Suit yourself.	隨你便。
Forget it.	別放在心上。／算了吧！／別管這個了。
What's the point?	那有什麼意義嗎?〔反話〕／重點是什麼?
Now you're talking.	這樣才對嘛。／這樣才像話嘛。

茱麗亞: 妳去過里奇蒙嗎?

伊 芙: 沒有。

茱麗亞: 那為什麼不和我一起回去? 我爸媽一定很高興妳來, 有
很多好玩的事情, 還有一流的越南餐廳喔, 來嘛, 跟我
們大家在一起。

伊 芙: 妳人真是太好了, 而且, 冬天去里奇蒙也算是淡季吧,
明天第一件事情就是打電話給我的旅行社。 (ring = call)

茱麗亞: 這樣才對嘛。

○ TIPS FOR EFFECTIVE COMMUNICATION ○

▶drive me up the wall 「真是不爽 (快把我逼瘋)」 drive a
person up the wall是口語上常用的片語, 意思是「惹惱, 使生氣,
使心神不寧」, 例如: Heavy traffic drives Luther up the wall. (交
通阻塞令路德心浮氣躁)。附帶一提, up如果改成to, 意思便變
成「逼入絕路, 使束手無策」, 兩者意義完全不同。

19 採買春酒飲料
DRINKS FOR AN AFTER-NEW YEAR'S PARTY

Ted: The next thing on the agenda for the party are the drinks.

Alden: 'Tis the season to be merry, fa la la la la, la la la la.

Ted: **Sober up.** This is planning and shopping time. We'll need wine and whiskey and beer.

Alden: But don't forget the mineral water crowd.

Ted: O.K. Now, what beer should we get? Some of those monster 3-liter sizes?

Alden: You mean Japanese beer?

Ted: **Why not?** Japanese beer is as good as the best of them.

Alden: I guess so. Nobody will know the difference anyway.

Ted: And wine, I suppose we should get some red and some white. Now you can get some decent Italian wines in 1.5 liter sizes and rather cheaply.

Alden: Why not Japanese wines?

Ted: **Come off it.*** Half of Japanese wine is mixed with some Algerian gunk and they don't have to put that on the label.

Alden: **Nobody will know the difference** anyway.

Ted: Don't be so cynical. A lot of people will know.

Alden: In a blindfold test, half the people probably couldn't distinguish between a red and a white.

泰德（34歲）是加拿大人，艾爾丹（36歲）則來自美國，兩人是東京一家國際學校的教師。寒假即將過去的一月上旬，兩人談起預定在二月中旬舉辦的教師新春派對。

食物的名單初步列好了，兩人開始討論需要準備哪些飲料，愛喝酒的兩個人從啤酒、葡萄酒、威士忌、伏特加、白蘭地、龍舌蘭，一路說到日本清酒，意見多得不得了。

泰　德：這次新春派對的下一件應辦事項是買喝的東西。

艾爾丹：這真是歡樂的好時光，呼啦啦啦～。《'Tis ～. = It is ～. 著名的耶誕聖歌當中的一小節》

泰　德：認真一點，現在是籌備和買東西的時候，我們需要葡萄酒、威士忌，還有啤酒。

艾爾丹：也別忘了喝礦泉水的人。

泰　德：好，那要買什麼啤酒？三公升裝的超大桶啤酒嗎？

艾爾丹：你說的是日本啤酒嗎？

泰　德：不好嗎？日本啤酒可是上等的啤酒呢。

艾爾丹：我想是吧，反正沒有人分得出來。

泰　德：還有葡萄酒，我想紅酒和白酒都要買一點，現在可以廉價買到還不錯的一點五公升裝義大利葡萄酒。《red = red wine》

艾爾丹：為什麼不買日本的葡萄酒？

泰　德：別說傻話了，日本的葡萄酒有一半都是和阿爾及利亞的劣等酒混著賣，而且又不用標示。

艾爾丹：反正又沒有人分得出來。

泰　德：少尖酸刻薄了，很多人都分得出來。

艾爾丹：如果把眼睛遮起來測驗，可能有一半的人根本都分不出來紅酒和白酒。

19

Ted: People know the difference.

Alden: I'll give you two to one that* if you poured the wine from a bottle with an expensive label and put it into a bottle with a cheap label, the majority would never know. They taste with their eyes.

Ted: I'll take you up on that. But not today. Today is a work day.

Alden: O.K. Japanese beer. Italian wine. And French mineral water. What about whiskey?

Ted: I hate Scotch. Why not get some Tennessee sour mash like Jack Daniel's?

Alden: Fine with me. But aren't we being a little bit self-centered here? You hate Scotch but millions love it.

Ted: Touché. And there's always vodka.

Alden: The Polish stuff, you know the vodka with some stalks of special grass inside it.

Ted: Well, **that should do it**. Otherwise there'll be no end.

Alden: Aren't we forgetting something?

Ted: What? Calvados? Tequila? **We've got to draw the line somewhere,** don't you?

Alden: I'll give you a hint. What else do people drink here besides beer and whiskey and wine?

Ted: Ah. Of course. Of course. Good old sake.

Alden: Right. Good old sake.

Ted: O.K. Sake's in.

Alden: We'll need something to drink it from.

Ted: What in tarnation are you talking about?

Alden: Well you wouldn't want to drink sake from a whiskey glass, now would you?

Ted: **Wouldn't faze me.**

泰　德：別人分得出來啦。

艾爾丹：我以二賠一跟你打賭，　假如你把一罐上面標價很貴的酒
　　　　從瓶子裡倒出來，　然後再注入標價很便宜的瓶子裡，　大
　　　　部分的人都分辨不出來，　他們不相信味覺，　只相信眼睛
　　　　看到的。《pour [por] 灌，倒》

泰　德：我會跟你賭，　不過要改天，　今天得辦正經事。

艾爾丹：好吧。日本啤酒、義大利葡萄酒，　還有法國礦泉水，　那
　　　　威士忌要買哪種？

泰　德：我討厭蘇格蘭威士忌，為什麼不買田納西的麥芽威士忌，
　　　　像是「傑克丹尼」啊？

艾爾丹：我都可以啦，　不過我們是不是有點兒太自我為中心了？
　　　　雖然你討厭蘇格蘭威士忌，　不過許多人可是愛得不得了。

泰　德：說得好，　而且少不了伏特加。

艾爾丹：買波蘭的好了，　就是那種酒瓶裡裝了特別的禾梗那種。
　　　　《the Polish stuff 波蘭出產的物品；此指波蘭產的伏特加》

泰　德：那好，　這樣就夠了，　再下去會沒完沒了。

艾爾丹：我們是不是忘記什麼東西？

泰　德：什麼東西？　法國蘋果白蘭地嗎？　還是龍舌蘭？　我們不是
　　　　應該就此打住了嗎？

艾爾丹：給你一個提示，　這裡的人除了啤酒、威士忌、葡萄酒之
　　　　外，　還會喝什麼酒？

泰　德：啊，　對啦，　陳年清酒。

艾爾丹：對，　陳年清酒。

泰　德：好，　日本清酒也加進來了。《～ be in 加入～》

艾爾丹：我們還得買一些酒杯。

泰　德：你在講什麼有的沒的？

艾爾丹：你喝清酒不會用威士忌酒杯對不對？

泰　德：我是沒差啦。《faze 困擾》

Alden: Let's get some of those little sake cups and a sake jug for heating it up.

Ted: Little sake cups and a sake jug? **What a pain.**

Alden: So what? It's a great conversation piece. And besides, maybe some people can't tell the difference between red and white wine or the difference between Japanese and German beer, and maybe some couldn't care less if the vodka's from Poland or Osaka, but you can bet your bottom dollar that everyone can tell the difference between Scotch on-the-rocks and hot sake!

關鍵句

Sober up.	認真一點。／嚴肅一點。
Why not?	為什麼不要？／不好嗎？
Come off it.	別說傻話了。／別瞎扯了。
Nobody will know the difference.	沒有人知道差別在哪裡。／不會有人分得出來的。
That should do it.	這樣就夠了。／那就這樣了。
We've got to draw the line somewhere.	我們該有個限度。
(It) Wouldn't faze me.	我沒差。／我不會覺得懊惱。
What a pain.	真是麻煩。

艾爾丹： 要買一些小酒杯，還有溫酒壺。

泰　德： 要買小酒杯還有溫酒壺喔？ 真是麻煩！

艾爾丹： 那又怎樣？ 一定會是全場的焦點話題， 你看， 可能有些人分不出來紅酒和白酒， 也分不出來日本啤酒和德國啤酒，還有些人不在意伏特加酒是波蘭產的還是大阪產的，但是你絕對可以打賭， 大家一定分得清楚加冰塊的威士忌和溫過的清酒差別在哪裡！《conversation piece 話題》

○ TIPS FOR EFFECTIVE COMMUNICATION ○

▶ **Come off it.**（口語）「少說傻話了」　come off it通常作命令形，意思是「少說笑了／少鬧了／少來這一套／不要騙了／少擺架子了」，和stop acting、stop pretending用法相同。例如：（兩位教師之間的談話） "Tomorrow is a school holiday. So I lose whole class."（明天學校放假，我一堂課都沒了） "Come off it! I'm sure you're as happy as I am that there's no class."（少來了！你一定和我一樣，高興不用上課。）

▶ **I'll give you two to one that ～**「我以二賠一跟你打賭（that以下的事）」　odds是「賭率、賠率」的意思，也可以寫成I'll give you odds of two to one [2 to 1].或是I bet you two to one.，意思是「如果你贏，我就給你兩倍的賭注」。看來，艾爾丹似乎很有把握。

20 店長難為
A MANAGER PUTS HIS FOOT IN HIS MOUTH

Mary: You look a little glum. What's the matter?

Keith: You really want me to tell you?

Mary: Sure. You know me. I'm the nosy type.

Keith: Boy, **am I in hot water**.

Mary: Why, what happened?

Keith: This morning we had a managers' meeting and someone proposed higher incentives for sales. I couldn't stomach another cash incentive; they're high enough so I suggested shorter hours.

Mary: And?

Keith: **I really put my foot in my mouth**.* That suggestion was the last thing anybody wanted to hear.

Mary: You could have said something worse such as "maybe we have too many managers."*

Keith: Are you trying to rib me?

Mary: Do you think **I** would **give** my boss **a lot of lip**? Believe me, if you ever need a helping hand, **I'll be by your side**.

Keith: Well, I can't help wondering if you've got the guts to stand up for me.

Mary: You think I'm lily-livered?

Keith: **I wouldn't say that** but I would say that sometimes when there's trouble, **I can't find hide or hair of you**.

> 　瑪麗（28歲）在美國科羅拉多州丹佛市一家運動用品店當店員，這是間連鎖店，店長是吉斯（37歲）。
> 　這天下午，吉斯開完店長會議回到店裡，瑪麗看他臉色不好，上前慰問，但似乎得到了反效果。

瑪　麗：你看起來有點悶悶不樂，怎麼了？

吉　斯：真的要講嗎？

瑪　麗：當然啦，你也知道我的個性，我就是愛管閒事嘛。

吉　斯：唉，我麻煩大了。

瑪　麗：怎麼了？發生什麼事？

吉　斯：今天早上有店長會議，有人提議我們應該提供更高的業績獎勵，但是我不能苟同，因為獎勵已經很高了，所以我建議縮短工時。《manager = store manager 店長》

瑪　麗：然後呢？

吉　斯：我簡直是拿石頭砸自己的腳，大家最不想聽到的就是這種建議。

瑪　麗：不會啊，還有更糟的，像是「也許店長人數太多了」之類的。

吉　斯：妳是在挖苦我嗎？

瑪　麗：你以為我會對自己的老闆放肆嗎？相信我，萬一有需要我幫忙的地方，我一定會支持你。

吉　斯：嗯，我還是懷疑妳是不是有勇氣站出來為我說話。

瑪　麗：你以為我是膽小怕事的人？

吉　斯：我不是這個意思，可是偶爾有麻煩的時候，我就是看不到妳的蹤影。

Mary: **That's not fair. That's below the belt.** Have I ever let you down?

Keith: Well, maybe not. But you've got a gift for staying out of the line of fire while I usually have to take it on the chin.

Mary: **That comes with the territory.**

Keith: Here I am trying to improve operations, trying to find new solutions. And what happens? I get shot down.

Mary: I can see your nerves are on edge.

Keith: Of course they are! And you're not making me feel any better.

Mary: Look. The meeting's over, right? **The dust is settled,** right? Relax. You can't win them all. And, by the way, what was finally decided? More cash incentives?

Keith: They're mulling it over. It'll probably be an extra five-dollars for every one-hundred dollars of sales in a given day.

Mary: On top of the other incentives we already have, that's not bad.

Keith: Not bad? We have so many cash incentives that our margins are getting paper-thin.

Mary: Things'll work out. I've been studying the long-range weather reports and it seems we're going to have lots and lots of snow so people will need lots and lots of skis and ski boots and ski jackets so we'll rack up lots and lots of sales. In short, we'll make you look good.

Keith: **I could use that.** Maybe if I show better results, they'd listen to me more at the meetings.

Mary: Sure they will. You're about the best manager they've got.

Keith: I'm glad somebody with a good head on her shoulders thinks so.

Mary: **You're** just a little **ahead of your time**.

瑪　麗：你這樣說很不公平，太傷人了，我有讓你失望過嗎？

吉　斯：嗯，或許沒有吧。可是通常當我在受苦受難時，妳就是
　　　　有隔岸觀火的「天賦」。

瑪　麗：這是店長分內的事啊。

吉　斯：我真的很想要改善營運狀況，很想要找出解決方法，結
　　　　果呢？被人拒絕了。

瑪　麗：看得出來你現在精神有點緊繃。

吉　斯：不緊繃才怪，結果妳卻沒有讓我比較好受。

瑪　麗：聽我說，會已經開完了，也塵埃落定了，對吧？放輕鬆，
　　　　你不可能討好每一個人。對了，那最後的決定是什麼？
　　　　更高的獎金鼓勵嗎？

吉　斯：他們考慮再三，可能是在指定日那天，每一百元的業績
　　　　再加五元的獎金吧。

瑪　麗：在現有的獎勵之外再加上這項獎金制度，真是不錯啊。

吉　斯：不錯？我們的獎金鼓勵太浮濫了，導致我們的盈餘少得
　　　　可憐。

瑪　麗：事情總會解決的。我已經研究了長期的天氣預報，好像
　　　　會一直、一直下雪，所以大家會用到許多許多的雪橇、
　　　　滑雪靴和滑雪夾克，我們就會累積好多好多的業績。簡
　　　　單地說，我們會讓你很有面子的。

吉　斯：我倒是可以利用這一點，也許如果我交出比較亮麗的成
　　　　績單，他們開會的時候就會比較聽我的。

瑪　麗：當然會啦，你可以說是他們最好的店長呢。

吉　斯：真高興聽到有頭腦的人這麼說。

瑪　麗：你只是走在時代前面一些而已。

20

《《《關鍵句》》》———————————————

I'm in hot water.	我麻煩大了。／處境艱難。
I put my foot in my mouth.	我拿石頭砸自己的腳。／我惹麻煩了。
I give ～ a lot of lip.	對～放肆。／對～說冒失話。
I'll be by your side.	我支持你。
I wouldn't say that.	我不是這個意思。／我不會這樣說。
I can't find hide or hair of you.	看不到你的人影。／連個鬼影子都看不到。
That's not fair.	這樣很不公平。
That's below the belt.	（這樣說）太傷人了。／不公平。
That comes with the territory.	那是分內（可能發生）的事。
The dust is settled.	塵埃落定。／事情明朗了。／水落石出。
I could use that.	我可以利用這一點。
You are ahead of your time.	你走在時代之前。／你（的想法）比時代還先進。

○ *TIPS FOR EFFECTIVE COMMUNICATION* ○

▶ I really put my foot in my mouth. 「我簡直是拿石頭砸自己的腳」 put one's foot in one's mouth是口語中所說的「搞砸」的意思。有什麼事比把自己的腳塞到嘴巴更難堪的事呢？大概沒有。附帶一提，不曉得你有沒有注意到，這課會話中用了許多身體部位來表現，例如：nose, stomach, rib, lip, hand, guts, liver, hide, hair, chin... 沒有?! 噢，My eye!（我的天哪!）。

▶ You could have said something worse such as "maybe we have too many managers." 「不會啊，還有更糟的啊，像是『或許店長的人數太多了』之類的」 瑪麗說這句話的用意是要安慰吉斯。諸如：could [couldn't] have ～, would [wouldn't] have ～或是should [shouldn't] have ～這類與事實相反的假設語氣，如果能夠多加熟練，會話才會更生動自然。例如："When I looked at Jane's painting, I said 'That looks okay.'"（我在看珍的畫作時，說了一句：「看起來不錯。」）"You could have said something nicer!"（你就不能說些好聽的嗎?） / I wouldn't have done it.（要是我就不會那麼做）。

COMPREHENSION QUIZZES

I. WHY EVERYBODY TALKS ABOUT THE WEATHER

1. Why does Shinji check the weather report?

　a. For no special reason.

　b. He's worried about catching cold.

　c. He hates to get his clothes wet.

2. One reason why everyone talks about the weather is

　a. it's interesting.

　b. it's easy to talk about.

　c. it influences the economy.

3. The season Wayne likes best is

　a. summer.

　b. fall.

　c. no particular season.

4. Wayne speaks Japanese

　a. fairly well.

　b. not very well.

　c. very poorly.

5. The wife of Shinji's friend

　a. is good at hiking.

　b. is good at making lunch.

　c. is good at English.

▶ ACTIVITY

　Write or explain what topic you find easy to talk about with a person you don't know well.

2. DO PRETTY GIRLS THINK JAPANESE BUSINESSMEN ARE BORING?

1. Linda is working in Japan
   a. teaching art.
   b. teaching English.
   c. guiding tourists.
2. The pastries in the coffee shop
   a. are homemade.
   b. are from a famous bakery.
   c. are rather expensive.
3. Linda works
   a. at a private school.
   b. at a university.
   c. at various companies.
4. After listening to Linda's complaints, Yoshiro is
   a. insulted.
   b. analytical.
   c. bored.
5. Linda seems to be
   a. having a good time with Yoshiro.
   b. bored with Yoshiro.
   c. hungry for pastries.

▶ **ACTIVITY**

Write or explain one way to make learning English more interesting.

3. ETHIOPIA IN WASHINGTON D.C.?

1. Rob's brother lives in
   a. Washington State.
   b. Ethiopia.
   c. the capital of the USA.

2. Rob and Sally couldn't decide which restaurant to go to because
   a. there were so many.
   b. there were so few.
   c. they were too sleepy.

3. They got a recommendation for a restaurant from a
   a. bookshop clerk.
   b. taxi driver.
   c. guide book.

4. Eating the food was a problem because
   a. you had to use floppy bread.
   b. it was too spicy.
   c. the bowl was very deep.

5. When James and Rob go out to eat, how often does James pay for both of them?
   a. Never.
   b. Rarely.
   c. Often.

▶ **ACTIVITY**

What food [for example: crab, escargot] or cuisine do you find difficult to eat and why?

4. MAYBE SUSHI ISN'T JAPANESEY TODAY

1. Avis does not want sushi because

    a. she isn't used to raw fish.

    b. she's eaten it in America.

    c. she can't use chopsticks.

2. When Keisuke first hears Avis ask for blowfish,

    a. he doesn't understand.

    b. he laughs.

    c. he is embarrassed.

3. The two don't eat blowfish because

    a. it's out of season.

    b. it's poisonous.

    c. it's too expensive.

4. Keisuke and Avis don't have loach because

    a. there's a language problem.

    b. there's not enough time.

    c. Avis does not care for such fish.

5. The main reason Avis finally agrees to have a Japanese steak

    a. is that it is unbelievably expensive.

    b. is that she does not want to eat whale.

    c. is to be polite.

▶ ACTIVITY

If you traveled to America and could only have one dish, explain what you would choose.

5. BUYING A CAR IN TOKYO

1. The two kinds of car transmissions are

    a. diesel and gasoline.

    b. automatic and manual.

    c. regular and special.

2. Putting the shift lever on the floor is

    a. usually impractical.

    b. usually makes driving safer.

    c. usually a good idea.

3. Retractable headlights is an example of

    a. irrational technology.

    b. rational technology.

    c. how to make cars more economical.

4. When it comes to air-conditioning, Jack thinks

    a. it's a necessity.

    b. it's nice to have.

    c. it's not often needed.

5. Don is surprised that Jack

    a. wants a used car.

    b. has no driver's license.

    c. has no parking place.

▶ ACTIVITY

Write or explain three points you would look for if you were going to buy a car.

6. PROBLEMS OF PURITY

1. When it comes to administrative details, John

    a. enjoys discussion.

    b. hates discussion.

    c. is accustomed to them.

2. John got his new dog

    a. from a dog shelter.

    b. from a kennel.

    c. from a friend.

3. Tsutomu is happy with his dog because

    a. it was expensive.

    b. it never gets sick.

    c. his wife is happy.

4. If a child's parents are Japanese and American, the best thing to call that child is

    a. Eurasian.

    b. half.

    c. mixed.

5. In the mornings,

    a. John walks the dog.

    b. John's wife walks the dog.

    c. Tsutomu walks the dog.

▶ ACTIVITY

If you have a pet, explain how you got it. If you don't have a dog, how would you get one?

7. DOES THE SUN RISE BY DIFFERENT RULES?

1. When it comes to the book *The Rising Sun*, Kathy

  a. has seen the movie.

  b. has read the book.

  c. has neither read the book nor seen the film.

2. The music for the movie was written by

  a. a famous Japanese composer.

  b. a famous Hollywood composer.

  c. a popular commercial composer.

3. When Suzanna went to school in America,

  a. there were probably few sushi shops.

  b. there were many sushi shops.

  c. people hated Japan.

4. Kathy's friend

  a. works for a Danish organization.

  b. works in Japan.

  c. loves cheese.

5. After their talk, the two

  a. go to a different bar for another drink.

  b. have another drink where they are.

  c. say goodbye and go home.

▶ ACTIVITY

Write or explain the image of America in any Chinese book or movie.

146

8. CRYSTAL CLEAR ANSWERS AREN'T ALWAYS THE BEST

1. George thought the main point of judo is

   a. to throw down your opponent.

   b. the spirit of judo.

   c. to watch experienced players.

2. George has been in Japan

   a. longer than Mat.

   b. not as long as Mat.

   c. about the same time as Mat.

3. In reply to George's first question, Mat

   a. says he doesn't know.

   b. gives a clear answer.

   c. gives no answer at all.

4. During the discussion, George

   a. becomes irritated.

   b. remains calm.

   c. becomes hungry.

5. To George, Mat's explanations seem

   a. very intelligent.

   b. complicated.

   c. rather clear.

▶ ACTIVITY

Give an example of a question with a yes / no answer, and an example of a question that has no yes / no answer.

9. HOW TO TALK ABOUT JAPANESE FOOD

1. When Noriko asks for Greg's help, Greg

   a. is unhappy.

   b. is happy.

   c. is angry.

2. If Noriko had brought a tape recorder,

   a. it would have been convenient.

   b. Greg would have been pleased.

   c. it would have been a problem.

3. Most non-Japanese

   a. like *natto* right away.

   b. need time to get used to *natto*.

   c. think it is a kind of cheese.

4. Describing how to eat miso-soup is

   a. difficult.

   b. easy.

   c. fun.

5. Greg wants Noriko to drink more beer because

   a. she is a strong drinker.

   b. she talks too much.

   c. she gets drunk easily.

▶ **ACTIVITY**

Pick any Chinese dish and explain how you would describe it to a person who knows nothing about it.

10. GAMBLING VS. INVESTING

1. If you withdraw money from a time deposit before maturity,

   a. you receive a lower rate of interest.

   b. you receive less money than you put in.

   c. you need your mother's permission.

2. The PE's of Japanese stocks are

   a. average.

   b. low.

   c. high.

3. In investing, Ralph seems to usually

   a. take no risks.

   b. accept moderate risk.

   c. prefer gold to time deposits.

4. Michio seems to know

   a. very little about investing.

   b. a lot about currency exchange.

   c. quite a bit about investing.

5. Ralph agrees with Michio so he will

   a. gamble 1.6 million on speed boat racing.

   b. gamble all his money on speed boat racing.

   c. put 1.6 million in a super-*teiki*.

▶ ACTIVITY

Write or explain exactly what you would do if you had $50,000.

149

11. DATING: TWO PEOPLE WHO HAVE LITTLE IN COMMON

1. Helen is

  a. not busy.

  b. moderately busy.

  c. very busy.

2. Andy would like to take Helen out

  a. next week.

  b. next weekend.

  c. today.

3. Andy's first suggestion is

  a. Chinese food.

  b. Italian food.

  c. Japanese food.

4. When Andy mentions three movies and asks Helen to choose, she

  a. tells Andy it's up to him.

  b. picks the French movie.

  c. picks the science-fiction movie.

5. *Shane* is a movie that

  a. Helen would like to see again.

  b. both would like to see but it's too far.

  c. Helen would not like to see again.

▶ **ACTIVITY**

Write or explain about problems you've had with friends in deciding where to go.

12. PROBLEMS OF THE MORNING RUSH IN TOKYO

1. When Leroy used to drive to work,

    a. he enjoyed the car's stereo.

    b. he arrived feeling fine.

    c. he arrived feeling tired.

2. Tim believes JR trains

    a. are terribly crowded.

    b. are getting better.

    c. are getting worse.

3. The new JR cars have

    a. more doors.

    b. bigger doors.

    c. fewer doors.

4. Leroy thinks that making more physical space is

    a. good in theory but bad in practice.

    b. bad in theory but good in practice.

    c. bad both in theory and in practice.

5. After their talk, Leroy is

    a. sure to switch from car to train.

    b. will not switch from car to train.

    c. does not know what to do.

▶ ACTIVITY

Write or explain any special tips for traveling more comfortably on public transportation.

13. HOW TO BE A GOOD GUY

1. Joy Cooper is coming from
   a. Osaka.
   b. New York.
   c. Chicago.

2. Dean is probably
   a. in his twenties.
   b. in his thirties.
   c. in his forties.

3. For this party, the company will
   a. pay all expenses.
   b. pay most expenses.
   c. pay about half the expenses.

4. Nagao will
   a. collect money at the door.
   b. pick the menu.
   c. meet Joy at Narita.

5. Joy probably
   a. does not know about the party.
   b. isn't interested in the party.
   c. is anxious about the party.

▶ ACTIVITY

Write or explain about some party or event you helped organize.

152

14. WHAT TO DO AT CHURCH

1. Miho has

   a. never been to church.

   b. been to church a few times.

   c. goes to church regularly.

2. In Grace's church

   a. only the same people come.

   b. new people often come.

   c. noisy children are not welcome.

3. Christian groups include

   a. Methodists.

   b. Jews.

   c. Muslims.

4. For Miho, religion is

   a. not important.

   b. quite important.

   c. a fad.

5. For church, Miho decides to wear

   a. jeans.

   b. kimono.

   c. formal dress.

▶ ACTIVITY

Write or explain about the first time you attended a meeting of a religious or social group.

15. THE PERENNIAL PROBLEM OF NARITA

1. Victor is going home for
   a. his wedding.
   b. his brother's wedding.
   c. his sister's wedding.

2. Going to Narita airport is something that Eric
   a. hates.
   b. enjoys.
   c. is indifferent to.

3. Finding the Narita Express platform at Tokyo Station is
   a. difficult.
   b. easy.
   c. fun.

4. The most important thing for Victor when choosing flights is
   a. price.
   b. convenience.
   c. comfort.

5. Eric tells Victor
   a. he'll drive Victor to Narita.
   b. to take a taxi to Narita.
   c. to take an early train to Narita.

▶ ACTIVITY

Write or explain any problem you have had in getting to an airport or train station.

16. *HISHAKU* AND CAMPING

1. Gary is

    a. still single.

    b. married and has children.

    c. like Daniel Boone.

2. When Kurt goes camping,

    a. he takes fancy foods.

    b. he takes only basic foods.

    c. he takes mainly instant foods.

3. Gary has

    a. a big tent and a small tarp.

    b. a small tent and a big tarp.

    c. a small tent and a small tarp.

4. A small table for a tent

    a. is practical.

    b. is useless.

    c. is space-consuming.

5. American outdoor catalogs

    a. never have *hishaku*.

    b. usually have *hishaku*.

    c. sometimes carry *hishaku*.

▶ **ACTIVITY**

Write or explain about how you have actually prepared for an outdoor activity.

17. THE VERY PINK OF A CONVERSATION

1. The season that Mark likes best is

   a. spring.

   b. fall.

   c. a quiet one.

2. Mark thinks that perhaps native American Indians

   a. are happy about Thanksgiving.

   b. ignore Thanksgiving.

   c. are unhappy about Thanksgiving.

3. For Thanksgiving, Philip eats

   a. canned whole cranberries.

   b. fresh cranberries.

   c. canned smooth-style cranberries.

4. "Turkey" and "lemon"

   a. both share a common meaning.

   b. make a good combination to eat.

   c. have absolutely nothing in common.

5. Mark and Philip seem

   a. to talk very little.

   b. have witty conversations.

   c. have average polite conversations.

▶ **ACTIVITY**

Write or tell about some word that has many possible different meanings.

18. IS OFF-SEASON MORE FUN?

1. Eve has not bought a plane ticket for the holidays because
  a. she has no money.
  b. she does not plan to leave.
  c. she is afraid of flying.

2. Eve thinks that the New Year holidays in Tokyo are
  a. enjoyable.
  b. boring.
  c. expensive.

3. Julia believes that traveling off-season
  a. is cheaper.
  b. isn't much fun.
  c. is exciting.

4. Julia's parents probably
  a. wouldn't want an unexpected guest.
  b. would be happy to have Eve stay.
  c. don't like Vietnamese food.

5. In the end, Eve decides
  a. to go with Julia to Richmond.
  b. to remain in Tokyo.
  c. to go to a fancy restaurant.

▶ ACTIVITY

Write or explain about the advantages of off-season travel.

19. DRINKS FOR AN AFTER-NEW YEAR'S PARTY

1. Alden is

    a. doubtful about Japanese beer.

    b. enthusiastic about Japanese beer.

    c. unhappy about 3-liter cans of beer.

2. Ted thinks that Japanese wines

    a. are quite good.

    b. are quite poor.

    c. are rather cheap.

3. According to Alden, most people

    a. can tell the difference between wines.

    b. prefer red wines.

    c. can't tell the difference between wines.

4. The drink that Ted has forgotten about was

    a. Calvados.

    b. vodka.

    c. sake.

5. Drinking sake from a whiskey glass

    a. wouldn't bother Ted.

    b. wouldn't bother Alden.

    c. is a good idea.

▶ ACTIVITY

Write or explain very specifically what drinks you think are suitable for an enjoyable party.

20. A MANAGER PUTS HIS FOOT IN HIS MOUTH

1. At the managers' meeting, Keith makes a suggestion that
   a. is welcomed by all.
   b. nobody understood.
   c. nobody liked.

2. If there is a problem, Mary is
   a. sometimes hard to find.
   b. always there and helpful.
   c. often the cause.

3. Keith thinks that cash incentives
   a. are a method that should be tried.
   b. are quite effective.
   c. reduce the company's profits.

4. Mary studies the weather reports
   a. because she likes outdoor sports.
   b. because it affects business.
   c. because it is her hobby.

5. Mary tries to give Keith
   a. a headache.
   b. support.
   c. secret information.

▶ **ACTIVITY**

Write or explain what method you think will motivate employees to work harder.

ANSWERS TO QUIZZES

1	1. a	2. b	3. b	4. b	5. c
2	1. b	2. a	3. c	4. b	5. a
3	1. c	2. a	3. a	4. a	5. b
4	1. b	2. a	3. a	4. b	5. a
5	1. b	2. a	3. a	4. a	5. c
6	1. b	2. a	3. c	4. a	5. b
7	1. c	2. a	3. a	4. a	5. a
8	1. a	2. b	3. a	4. a	5. b
9	1. a	2. c	3. b	4. a	5. c
10	1. a	2. c	3. b	4. c	5. a
11	1. b	2. c	3. a	4. a	5. a
12	1. c	2. b	3. a	4. a	5. c
13	1. c	2. b	3. b	4. b	5. a
14	1. a	2. b	3. a	4. a	5. b
15	1. b	2. a	3. a	4. a	5. a
16	1. b	2. a	3. b	4. a	5. a
17	1. a	2. c	3. a	4. a	5. b
18	1. b	2. a	3. b	4. b	5. a
19	1. a	2. b	3. c	4. c	5. a
20	1. c	2. a	3. c	4. b	5. b

英語大考驗

想知道你的文法基礎夠紮實嗎？你以為所有的文法概念，老師在課堂上都會講到嗎？由日本補教界名師撰寫的《英語大考驗》，提供你一個思考英語的新觀點，不管是你以為你已經懂的、你原本不懂的、還是你不知道你不懂的問題，在這本書裡都可以找到答案！

English test

活用美語修辭
——老美的說話藝術

日常生活中，我們經常引用各種譬喻，加入想像力的調味，使自己的用字遣詞更為豐富生動，而英語的世界又何嘗不是？且看作者如何以幽默的筆調，引用英文書報雜誌中的巧言妙句，帶您倘佯美國人的想像天地。

21 世紀英語學習貴在理解，而非死背

自然學習英語動詞
基礎篇

本書幫助您不需過度依賴文字解釋，就能清楚區分每個字彙特有的語感，切實掌握各個字彙不同的含義。進而使讀者能深切體會意象的道理，加以融會貫通，確實將英文字彙靈活運用在實際會話中。

English test

That's It!
就是這句話！

簡單、好記正是本書的一貫宗旨，們知道您有旺盛的學習慾，但是有候，真的，心不要太大，把一句記到熟就夠了！